# The Last Magi
## *A Christmas Tale*

by E. A. Sharpe

Positive Imaging, LLC
Austin, Texas

Printed in the United States of America
First Edition, 2015

ISBN 978-1-944071-02-8

*For Margaret,*
*always for Margaret*

# Table of Contents

# Chapter One

## The Star in the East

BEHOLD, in the East rose a star where no star had been, shining in the sign of the dragon, brighter than any in the night sky. In palaces and huts and roads, high and low alike turned their heads to the heavens and were amazed, for it had bloomed nine nights before and each night traveled westward toward... what? All agreed it was a portent, but of good or ill, no one knew.

Now this was in the thirty-first year of the reign of Augustus, Emperor of Rome, and the fifth year of Herod, King of Judea and the twelfth of Mithradates, ruler of Persia. In Persia's great trading city of Ecbatana, a tall man in a turban and purple robe stood at the window of a high tower, gazing thoughtfully at the light. On his breast hung a winged circle of gold, emblem of his order. A servant handed him a long brass cylinder and the man put it to his eye to better inspect this heavenly visitor.

In all the city he was the only person who had such an instrument, for he was a longtime student of the stars. And also was he a Mage, one of the Magi, a priest of the prophet Zoroaster, who revealed the faceless god whose emblem is fire. His name was Artaban and although his beard was not yet long or white, he was counted high in that order of holy and learned men. He had traveled to many foreign lands and spoke many tongues. Like his brothers, he taught the words of Zoroaster, and also was he wise in astrology and numbers and the healing arts.

"What do you see in the magic looker, Master?" asked the servant, who knew better than to bother his employer with questions but was too young to contain himself.

His master answered not and in the flickering light of a brazier, the boy studied the face of the man who studied the star. He had keen gray eyes and a prominent nose with a high brow and thin, fine lips. A trim, black beard bordered his features. Together they gave him the aspect of one who is both a mystic and soldier – who sees far and has the courage to venture as far as he may see.

At length the Mage took the glass from his eye. "This is not magic, Fashid."

"Your looker brings close things that are far away," said the boy. "What is that but magic?"

"Its glass is ground to make far away things *look* close. That is no more than optics and don't ask me about optics for I haven't the time. As to what I see, you may judge for yourself."

The boy took the telescope and through it saw a bright dancing diamond with light streaming behind it like long strands of heavenly hair. "Is it alive?" he asked.

"No, though it is a manifestation of the faceless god, a brightly burning ball of fire. It is moving through the sky. In a few weeks it will be gone."

"What does it mean, Master? Is it good or bad?"

"For you and most of this city, Fashid, it likely means very little either way. But it may someday mean much to those who sit on thrones. If I was such a one, especially in Rome or Jerusalem, and I understood the message of this light, I'd be uneasy about my line."

"An usurper? You mean someone to take their thrones? Will he chop off their heads?"

"Not so loud, lad! Even here, high above the street, it is unwise to talk of tossing throne-sitters, even distant ones. As to what the one who comes will do and how he will do it, I can't say. All I know is my part in his story."

"And what is that, Master?"

"I must find him."

# Chapter Two

## Rasha

"WHAT is this you must find?" said grey-bearded Tigranes, who reclined on pillows with his wife Mashid and his eldest daughter Rasha. "A fallen star? This is a child's tale, Artaban. Have you lost your mind?"

"The star has not fallen, venerable Tigranes," said Artaban, who sat before the three on a pillow of his own. "It but points the way."

"And what way is that?"

"Westward. I go in search of a ruler born in the West."

They were in Tigranes' private chambers, a sumptuous room of thick fringed carpets, walls of mahogany and olivewood and hangings of rich cloth. Incense perfumed the afternoon air.

Tigranes was a merchant of standing and wealth with three sons and four daughters. Mashid and Rasha silently sat a respectful distance from the two men, their heads covered in bright silk scarves. The servants had departed and the door shut. The four were alone, though Rasha's three sisters stood on the door's other side, ears pressed to the wood.

"In the West? That's all you know?" said Tigranes with exasperation. "This ruler, does he have a name?"

"He has not been born yet."

"Not born yet!" snorted the other.

"The star is the sign of a prophecy foretold by the Chaldean sage Balaam, son of Beor." Artaban took from his robe a parchment and read aloud. *"There comes a star out of Jacob and a scepter shall arise in Israel."*

"Israel is a nation of grovelers," harrumphed the portly merchant. "The Babylonians made slaves of them. So did the Egyptians. So did we once upon a time. Now the sons of Jacob and the rest of the tribes are scattered like sheep on the mountain."

"There is a remnant in Judea."

"Ruled by a puppet of Rome. Balaam son of Beor was a lunatic if he thought that star or scepter should ever rise from there. And you are a lunatic if—"

"Father!" cried Rasha with heat. Her mother put a hand on the girl's arm.

Tigranes looked with amusement at his child, then turned back to Artaban. "As I was about to say, none but a lunatic would set off for such a hazy figment less than a month from his wedding day." He grinned and gestured at Rasha. "Look at your bride to-be, young man. What a prize! Sixteen years old and wise beyond her years. Bold, too, unafraid to express her seasoned opinion about everything under the sun, don't I know it! You see how she stands up to the fearsome Tigranes, tiger of the marketplace. Already she's cast her lot with you. Right now she's wrapped up so all you can see of her are her hands and ankles and face, but look upon that face. A flower, no?"

Artaban gazed at the girl. A single strand of black hair had escaped the red scarf that framed her olive face, dangling just over a pair of modestly lowered eyes which were fringed by lush lashes. Gold loops hung from her shell ears. At that moment her rosy lips were carefully free of expression but Artaban had seen them at other times, when they formed a slim smile of beguilement or puckered in a pretty pout or spread wide in merriment. He thought he would never tire of the myriad ways they wordlessly conveyed her ever shifting moods.

"I look,' he said softly. "And what I see is beauty beyond compare."

"Wait till you compare it to the rest of her!" chortled her father. Rasha blushed and her mother glowered at Tigranes, who ignored her stare. "When you find out what she's like under all that swaddling, you won't want to leave your home for the sun and moon and all the stars in the Milky Way! She's a housekeeper who'll keep your home in order. A cook who'll make you plump as a pasha. She'll bear you stalwart sons and warm your wick—"

Tigranes broke off when Mashid's glare grew so fierce he could no longer pretend not to notice. "As I was about to say, she'll keep you warm on cold nights. Artaban, I'm an old man, old enough to be your father. I wed late in life and now that I'm married, I regret every day I spent making money when I could have been begetting babies. Don't put off the pleasures of family like I did. Children are sweet at any age but sweeter when you're young enough to carry them on your back."

Artaban took his gaze from the face of Rasha and spoke slowly. "This is no rash decision. There are other prophecies. Nor am I the only one who has watched for this light. A year ago I met with three brother priests from other cities: Balthazar, Melchior and Caspar. We compared our findings and forged a plan."

"And what is that?"

"We agreed if the wandering star appeared, we would watch it for ten days to determine its path. This is the tenth and it clearly points to the West. Eleven days from now I will join my friends at the Temple of Fire near Babylon and together we'll journey to find the infant born to rule."

"Journey *where?*" exclaimed Tigranes. "Much land lies west of Babylon."

"The star points to Jerusalem. We will go there and seek word of him."

"Jerusalem! It takes one of my caravans months to reach that hovel of stink and sin."

"Caravans are slow. I have Vasda, the swiftest mare in Persia. She will carry me to Babylon in ten days, eleven at most."

"Yes, one man on a fast horse might do that, but desert lands lie between Babylon and Jerusalem. You and your friends will have to trade your mounts for camels, and no one gallops through the desert. Even if you should find this child your first day in Jerusalem, which you won't, you'll never make it back on the day we set."

"This is why I'm here, revered Tigranes, to beg forgiveness for this sudden departure and to ask your daughter to wait until my return."

"I w—" began Rasha, but her mother slapped her wrist and she fell silent.

"In matters of my daughter's heart, my daughter is not the one you must beg," announced Tigranes. "I am sole arbiter of her future." He bent to sip from his cup and his eyes met Mashid's, whose chin dipped slightly. He returned his gaze to the Mage. "Artaban, when I contract with a man, I expect him to keep his part of the bargain. Why didn't you bring this matter up when we set the wedding date?"

"That was months ago and I was doubtful the star would appear, at least this year. When it did, I kept hoping it would fade before its meaning was certain. Believe me, worthy Tigranes, I did not want to put off my wedding either."

"I should hope not! So you are determined to carry out with this mad quest?"

"I am."

The gaze of Tigranes once again wandered to his wife, whose lips framed a silent syllable. "Then I suppose Rasha must wait until you return."

"If I may speak, father?" said Rasha.

"Go ahead, daughter."

"We needn't put off the wedding. There is a way for Artaban to marry me and still follow his star."

"Short of a flying carpet, I should like to hear it."

"We can marry today."

Mashid gasped but Tigranes only arched his eyebrows. "A practical solution, but then you are a practical girl. Sadly, child, Artaban's journey is long and dangerous. What if, terrible thought, he dies of disease or bandits or mishap? Worse, what if, as travelers sometimes do, he vanishes? Bad enough to be a widow, worse to be a widow without the certainty of widowhood. You couldn't remarry."

"Then I will go with him and have the certainty that whatever befalls him will befall me as well."

Tigranes grinned and turned to Artaban. "My child and don't I know it! Quick-witted and plucky. True, no respecter of propriety or tradition but at her age, that's to be expected. What a prize! How can you turn your back on such devotion?"

"I do not turn my back on your daughter, Tigranes. I only set aside the pleasures of marriage that I might behold the fruit of prophecy." He turned to the girl. "Rasha, much am I moved by your readiness to go with me, but this is no journey for a female."

"He speaks true, daughter," said Tigranes. "I would think twice before I let any of your brothers set out, much less one of my flowers. Besides that, I can't let you marry without the pomp that belongs to your station."

"My station matters not to me, father," declared Rasha.

"Ah, but it matters greatly to your mother and me. Only families without standing marry their children without ceremony. I am a prominent man and the wedding of my firstborn daughter is an occasion for celebration, particularly when it's to a man of such learning and position. Our friends and relatives, all sorts of important people, should be here to witness it. I know that at your age waiting is hard, but wait you must."

Tigranes turned to Artaban. "Follow your star, Mage. Find, if you can, the scepter that will rise from that downtrodden tribe and their ludicrous god. But whether your prophecy is true or false, hurry back."

"I will!"

"Rasha will wait until you return – or until we have word you will never return. May the sun smile on your journey."

Artaban rose and tugged his forelock before the older man, then bowed low to Mashid and her daughter. He turned and strode quickly to the door so that his face would not betray his pain, flinging it open to the shrieks of Rasha's sisters, who vanished with flurrying footsteps.

OUTSIDE the merchant's house, Artaban went through the gate and into the street, which like that of every big city was full of people in motion, walking briskly on business that would not wait, driving mule-drawn carts and wagons full of goods that would not keep, riding horses and chariots with news that would not hold. Up and down the street soldiers marched, beggars slouched, thieves slunk, elders hobbled, servants bustled. None tarried, for to tarry was to allow that your task was not urgent – or worse, that in this town full of people doing deeds and sometimes misdeeds, you had nothing to do at all.

"Pray tarry, sir," said a hunched figure that appeared before Artaban ere he'd gone two blocks. The speaker was a peddler child in a drab shawl with a basket of over-ripe fruit, her face hidden by the folds of a coarse gray scarf.

"Not today, girl," said Artaban brusquely. "I have business."

A hand clutched at his sleeve. "You are Artaban the Mage?"

He paused. "I am."

"I have a message for you," she said in a low voice, head bent awkwardly to the cobbles, like one born with a deformity.

"From whom?" Artaban demanded. "Who sent you?"

For answer, the other only withdrew into the shadows of an alley between brick buildings. Artaban followed, though not without putting his hand on the blade in his belt, for even priests of Zoroaster may have enemies.

"What is your message?" he demanded. "Be quick."

The peddler unbent and stood fully erect, turning her head so that her dark brown eyes met his own. "*I* am the message."

"Rasha!" he gasped. "What are you doing here?"

"I must speak with you. My father said I would wait until you return. But I know him and if you are not back in a year, he will let it be known suitors are welcome."

"And if I am not, so he should. But I *will* be back. In two months at the outside."

"I cannot w —"

"You *can* wait and you must. And if you are about to beg me to take you away, the answer is 'no.' I will not betray your parents. We must be properly wed, as in time we shall. But now I *will* take you home so you can slip inside before you're missed. Properly, I should take you to your father, but I can't betray one with such spirit."

"I wasn't about to ask you to take me," she said hotly. "You're far too *proper* to boldly whisk me off, don't I know it! What I came to tell you is that, whatever Papa said, I'll play old maid for no man! In a fortnight it will be the shortest day of the year. I will wait six months more, until the longest day. Then I'll tell my mother I can wait no longer. She'll scold but she'll come around and she will tell my father. And he, after much harrumphing, will give in to her, as he always does. And if you come back a year from now, you will not find me in my father's house, in a quiet room weaving and sighing. No, you must look for me in a house of my own, with servants of my own, my belly swelling with the child of a man who knows I am not a maiden to wait till he finds it convenient to marry."

Artaban was not accustomed to such blunt speech from a mere girl. His brows came together and he folded his arms. "I see that when we are husband and wife, we both will have much to learn."

"Such as?"

"For your part, you must learn propriety and obedience and when to hold that ever-quick tongue."

"And for your part?"

"I must learn to be patient till you're learned your part."

Her eyes flashed and Artaban saw her lips express a mood he'd not seen before, a stormy one. "Patience is something you have in plenty, greybeard. I'd sooner have a suitor with too little than too much."

"Now *that* is untrue!"

"What? That you're too patient?"

"Not that. I may be double your age but there is not a gray hair on my head."

"Ah, but there is," she smiled, reaching out a finger to touch the tip of Artaban's beard. A quick pluck and she held out a pepper strand. "There, now no one can call you 'greybeard.' At least until you grow another."

Artaban frowned fiercely to cover up his smile. "Once married to you, I'm sure I'll have others."

Her mouth curved in a new expression. "And I'll pluck every one, so that you stay dark-haired and handsome."

Now Artaban didn't try to hide his smile. "You mock me but you keep your own hair unfairly hidden. What color is it?"

"See for yourself," said Rasha. Her hands threw off the coarse scarf, revealing a pinned pillowy mass of hair black as a moonless sky. She pulled out one, two... three pins, then quickly shook her head. The hair unfurled behind her, a tumble of nightfall, falling over her shoulders and curling about her cheeks.

Artaban stood speechless, overwhelmed by both her brazenness and the voluptuous beauty of her raven hair.

"Drink your eyes full, betrothed," said she. "You'll not see it again until we've wed. Think on me cold nights as you bump along on your bony camel after your cold old star." She lifted the scarf. "And now I must run h—"

Artaban stepped forward, reaching a hand behind her head and another around her shoulders. He pulled her to him and crushed his mouth against hers. His hand clutched a knot of thick hair at the back of her neck and held it tight, as a man might a rope drawing him to a ship from a stormy sea.

Or perhaps drawing him into a stormy sea, for rescue from such roiling waters was something he didn't want. His restless, questing mind was for once still and his heart ruled his body – or his body his heart. Heart and body, in truth neither seemed in charge, both in thrall to the soft, slender creature held in his arms, rosy lips in an olive face, black hair twining and winding about him, mouth—when not against his own—issuing little gasps and murmurs and moans as his lips roved her cheeks, ears, chin, neck, lips again, Her body folded against him, her soft, giving flesh pressing against his hard, straining muscles. He felt sweat trickle beneath his robes and wanted nothing so much as to feel her skin against his. At that moment, he wanted nothing else: no ancient scroll, no roving star, no prophecy revealed. What did he care of sacred teachings, eternal wisdom? Here with this woman in his arms, him in hers, here was eternity enough.

And so they tarried for brief sweet minutes in a narrow alley off a crowded street in a great metropolis. The busy world flowed past them and, intent on its own matters, noticed them not.

Nor did they notice the world.

"RASHA! Rasha!" shrieked a small, thin voice.

Suddenly the girl pulled away from him, her eyes wide with alarm at sight of a pig-tailed child standing beside them.

"Homa!" she cried. "What are you doing here?"

"Nomi said to tell you Papa's looking for you. Why did you take off your scarf, Rasha?"

"Brat! You followed me!"

"No, no! I swear!"

"Then how did you find me?"

"Sholeh followed you. I followed her."

"And where is Sholeh?"

"Here, Rasha," said pigtails on the other side of them. "Where is your scarf?"

"And Nomi, where is she?"

"Back home, following Papa."

Despite himself, Artaban broke into laughter. "The house of Tigranes holds few secrets from your sisters!"

Rasha bound her hair in a hasty knot. "I must be gone."

"You dropped your basket, Rasha," said Homa. "The fruit's all spilled."

"Pick it up then," said Sholeh.

"*You* pick it up!"

"Hush, you two," said Rasha, pulling the gray scarf over her head. "Both of you pick up the fruit." She turned to Artaban. "And you, my betrothed, you must be gone too. You have a long journey ahead."

"And now it will seem longer," sighed Artaban.

"The figs are smushed, Rasha. Do you want them anyway?"

Rasha knotted the scarf beneath her chin and pressed herself against him with a sad smile. "Go find whatever's under your cold old star, greybeard." She kissed his lips, then quickly pulled away. "Find it soon and hurry home to me!"

She turned to her sisters. "Give me the basket. Come, you two, this way!"

They ran off, threading through the crowded street. Artaban watched them go. Rasha glanced back once, then they were lost to sight. He sighed and turned to make his own way home.

# Chapter Three

## Three Treasures

THE starry canopy was paling, its lanterns one by one extinguished, all but the westward moving star, now itself barely visible. Artaban stood on the terraced roof of his house clad in traveling garb, warming his hands over the coals of a brazier and chewing a bitter nut that chased sleep.

A thin, dignified man with a shaven head appeared holding a small cedar box. "I have brought your treasures, Master," said Jabar, oldest of his servants and steward of the house.

Artaban opened the lid and withdrew a ruby. He held it in two fingers and they watched the jewel catch the first rays of the sun, red as a glowing coal. "What do you think, Jabar?"

Jabar handed his master a small silk purse. "Magnificent. Worthy to be worn on the hand of a prince."

Artaban slipped the gem into the purse. He dipped into the box again and withdrew a sapphire that gleamed with a blueness deep as a bay at dawn. "What of this one?"

"Fit for the crown of a king."

Artaban put the second stone into the purse and once more put his hand in the box, this time taking out a pearl. He held it in his palm and they gazed on its perfect roundness and creamy shine. "And this?"

Jabar shut the lid of the cedar box. "Truly, it might adorn the ear of a sea god. To whom do you bring these jewels?"

Artaban put the pearl in his purse. "For one not yet born, a prince who will someday be king, ruler of nations and calmer of troubled waters."

"Truly?"

"So say the prophecies."

"Ruler of what nations?"

"Alas, that is hidden. I will join my fellow Magi in Borsippa and together we will find him. When we do, his lineage may answer the question."

"Lineage?"

"Yes, surely such a one will be highborn. Is everything ready?"

"Everything. In your saddlebags is a pouch with your healing herbs and unguents. Also food for twelve days."

"Water?"

"Two skins that will last three days, which you won't need. Many are the streams between here and Borsippa."

"My glass, have you packed it?"

"In your saddlebags." He handed Artaban a broad leather belt. "Here is a money belt to wear under your garments, lambs wool on the inside so not to chafe. It has five pockets, one for your jewels and four others for traveling money. You have twenty gold darics and fifty half-darics. You also have a hundred pennies, since common people will not have change for even a half-daric. This will suffice you even if you are gone a year."

Artaban put the purse in a pocket of the belt and then fastened it around his waist. "The daughter of Tigranes has decreed I must be back sooner. Let us pray to the One that I am. What else?"

"Your route. You have spoken to Ka-mal and Hakim?"

"I have. I will keep to the king's road most of the way, but I leave it to cross the Nisaean Plains and again after at the Brow of Darius."

Jabar handed his master two sheets of calfskin parchment. "Jabar has drawn a map to guide you across the plains. Hakim has done the other."

Artaban tucked away the two maps. "Then I have all I need. Is Vasda saddled?"

"Saddled and watered and impatient to be off."

"No doubt. She lives to run. A horse like no other! Do you remember that story you told me when I was little?"

"You mean 'How the One Made the Arabian?' I remember that and how big your eyes got at the thought of such a steed."

"All my life I yearned to own a mount so fleet. And when Ka-mal showed me the skinny colt he'd just bought—"

"You told him he'd spent your money on a swindle."

"That's why he is Stable Master and I am merely a star gazer. She's worth more to me than all three of these gems. But enough of this, Jabar. It's time I was off."

"Master, once more I beg you to take Hakim with you. It's unsafe to travel with such treasure."

"Unsafe to openly travel with such treasure. Clad as I am, I'm just another traveler. Riding with big Hakim, others would know I have something to guard. Besides, Vasda can outrun any horse in Persia."

"I will pray to the One that she never need do so. When may we expect your return, Master?"

"Look for me in the month of Mithra, around the time when the days and nights are equal. At least that is when I hope to be back. Sooner if I can. The stars take no heed of the doings of men but for me, the Chaldean's prophecy is inopportune. I'm anxious to return and make my betrothed mistress of this house."

"Well do I remember the sound of you and your cousins playing hide and seek and the lullabies of your mother as she sang you to sleep. Great happiness would it bring me to hear again the laughter of children and a woman in song."

Artaban embraced his steward. "Then let us pray the star guides my comrades and me truly. Then can I spur Vasda back and make happy my bride, myself and all who live beneath this roof!"

And with a high heart, he went down to the stable where Vasda impatiently waited, she born of Dol, sired by Trom, descendant of the war horses who pulled the chariot of Cyrus, she proud and beautiful in motion, who let none on her back but Artaban. Fourteen hands she stood. Her skin was roan, her mane brown, her eyes black, her nostrils wide and flaring. Her chest was broad, her back strong, her hooves quick, and high she carried her head and tail.

Artaban waited in the yard as Ka-mal, lame but wise in horse lore, led her from the stall. At sight of her master, the mare snorted crossly, as if to say, *"Laggard! Why have you kept me waiting? Don't you know we have a journey? No more dallying! Mount me and take me out that I may humble the wind and devour the road. Where are we bound? Never mind! North, south, east, west — all are the same to me, dust under my hooves. Point me. Hold tight my reins, hug me with your legs and hold on dearly, for I am Vasda, who flies without wings!"*

So Artaban placed his boot in the stirrup and swung into the saddle and took the reins from Ka-mal. He raised his hand in farewell and was about to spur his steed off but by then they were out of the yard and into the street and well past the houses of his neighbors and halfway through the city as he hung on dearly and Vasda raced to overtake the dawn.

# Chapter Four

## Vasda the Swift

THE SUN rose red on the horizon and mist lifted lazily from the land as birds chorused their morning praise. On the king's road, a carter and his sons drove their oxen through the outskirts of Ecbatana. The keen-eyed younger boy spotted the horseman first, barely a speck far ahead. Half a minute more and the carter himself could see the rider, small and distant but coming fast. They trundled past an old grain mill and the boy said the horseman was now within bowshot if he but had his bow. His brother laughed and said perhaps the mighty Arash of legend could shoot a bolt so far but not a skinny ten year-old. The other rejoined that had his bow, he would show the doubter how far he could shoot. His brother jeered and the boy flailed at him and he flailed back and their father told them to leave off and be quiet, but he couldn't be heard above the clatter of hooves as the rider and his mount thundered past.

The three turned their heads to gaze at the traveler, swallowed in a cloud of dust and already grown small. The carter allowed he must be one of the king's messengers to ride a steed so fleet. He must carry urgent news.

"What news, Papa?" asked the younger boy.

"We'll never know," said the carter. "The news of kings never comes to the low."

BY AFTERNOON Artaban had reached the high road that skirted the base of Mount Orontes and now he trotted Vasda along its rocky slopes, deeply furrowed by the torrents of past springs. One hundred and fifty parasangs must he ride to his appointed meeting. On Vasda he could cover fifteen parasangs a day, though he must needs rise before the sun and continue past its setting. Nine more days like today, he thought, and he would join his brothers at the temple of fire in Borsippa with a day to spare.

From there the four Magi would travel by camel, but all that would be already arranged by Balthazar and the others. Vasda he would board in Babylon with a cousin of Ka-mal's who stabled mounts for the royal family. It troubled him to leave her but the desert was no place for horses. Besides, the ride to Borsippa would be hard, even for a creature in her prime. The stay would give her ample time to rest and recover, a dry barn and fresh hay. She liked her morning apple! He must tell the cousin to see she got one, and also a chunk of honeycomb each afternoon. Ka-mal chided him for spoiling her but who else had he to spoil?

Well, perhaps a year from now he would be spoiling a squalling babe, that and pacifying a young wife with a temper like a teapot, ready to spout at any moment. She would not put up with a husband who spent nights on the roof. *"Come to bed! Leave your cold old stars and come to bed, Artaban. They'll be waiting for you tomorrow night. I may not!"*

A new life awaited him on his return. New demands, new distractions, new pleasures for an old bachelor. Good that Vasda would be rested and ready when his quest was done. Weary he would surely be, yet he might ride her hard and fast all the way home.

DESCENDING the foothills of Orontes, man and beast left the king's road for the plains of the Nisae-ans, waves of tall grass rippling in the wind, great squawking flocks of brown prairie birds bursting skyward at their approach. Artaban navigated by landmarks on Ka-mal's map: the stony-fingered crag, the patch of woods, the hill with the tumbled-down cairn. They met no travelers, unless one counted the herds of wild horses that traveled beside them in apparent curiosity at the strange animal—half horse, half man—that crossed their land. Vasda tossed her head in contempt at these country creatures that had never known a stable, never seen a city, never trod on cobbles or tasted hay. *Bumpkins!*

The next morning they rejoined the king's road and traversed the fertile fields of Concabar, grain house of Persia. Long rows of stooped threshers crossed the fields, swinging great scythes, the blades swishing through the air to slice the stalks. The hum of their work could be heard from the road. Wagons followed after the workers to gather and carry the cut stalks to stone threshing-floors where they were trampled by plodding donkeys, the first of many steps to turn grain into flour. The grain dust from the threshing-floors filled the air with an amber haze, so thick that it half-hid the great temple of Astarte with its four hundred pillars.

Two days later, the fifth day, they reached Baghistan, pretty town nestled in a rocky range of low mountains. Sore tempted was the traveler to rest a night in one of its famed hospitality houses with their sumptuous meals, downy beds, baths fed by hot springs and fragrant gardens green from snowmelt, but the star beckoned and he pressed on.

The sun was already on the decline when he came to the Brow of Darius, a high cliff with a relief of that mighty king, his foot on the neck of a fallen foe. Graven beside him was a list of his wars: Scythia, Thrace, Ionia, Pelusium – famous conquests known to every boy, never to be forgotten!

Artaban paused to consult Hakim's map. He nudged Vasda from the road and they picked their way across the steep slopes, threading through ranks of high pines toward a nameless pass that would cut a day off their journey. They reached it an hour before nightfall, only to find it blocked by an avalanche. He could climb over but Vasda never.

There was no choice but to turn back. Just before dark Artaban found an almost-level spot on the slope with a windbreak of fallen pines. From his saddlebags he took a pouch and poured a small cone of black China Powder. He cut pine shavings over it then used his flint to strike a spark. The powder erupted with a small explosion and lit the shavings. He added kindling and then pine branches and finally dragged several heavy limbs onto the blaze, which crackled merrily, casting warmth and light. Just in time too, for a moment later he heard the first wolf howl.

He unsaddled Vasda and rubbed her down. He neither hobbled nor tethered her for he knew she would not roam out of the firelight and though he doubted the wolves would attack, he wanted her to have full use of her legs and hooves. She fed on pine needles and bark while he ate bean mash and dates. He chewed the beans that chased sleep to keep him awake, lest he let the fire go low. His star was hidden on the other side of the slope and for the first night since it appeared he did not look upon it. He felt a strange pang, as one misses a valued companion, so much had it become the guidepost for this bend of his life.

Someday he would look back on his life's bends and twists, boring his grandchildren with an old man's memories. This one would interest them more than most, an adventure outside scrolls and star lore. By that time the ruler found by him and his fellows would likely sit on a throne – or thrones. Would he be all that the prophecies promised? Maybe, or perhaps he would come to naught. Prophecies had been known to fail. He suspected that happened more often than not. Predictions that come to pass are recorded and remembered. Failed ones are forgotten.

The wolves howled and prowled and sometimes he could see their hungry eyes just outside the firelight. Vasda was too proud to show her fear but the tremble in her legs told him she was afraid. He stroked her and sang her songs: his mother's lullabies, tender ballads, tavern tunes, whatever came to mind.

He told her, as Jabar had once told him, how the One made the Arabian. "So seeing that in his creation there was nothing fleet and beautiful, he took a handful of south wind and another of running water and molded them, saying, 'I create thee, O Arabian. To thy forelock, I bind victory in battle and upon thy back I heap its spoils. To thy loins I confer might and fury, and to thy legs speed like no other. Much am I pleased with thee, for thou art one of the glories of this earth. Let all gaze and marvel, for I give thee flight without wings!'"

So the two passed the night, sometimes wakeful, sometimes lightly dozing. Artaban wrapped his cloak about him and leaned against a tree. Vasda's whinny woke him with a start to see the fire had burned into coals, but by then sunbeams pierced the pines. A few minutes later the mare was saddled and they were on their way.

IT WOULD take the morning to make it back to the road. This folly would cost them a full day. Bitterly, Artaban took out the map and cast it to the wind. *Hakim, why did you draw me a shortcut that does not exist?* After a hour of stewing, he reminded himself he was a Mage, full of wisdom and above such childish pettiness. He might as well blame the calf who provided the skin for the map. Or the cow who gave birth to the calf. Or the farmer who owned the cow. Or the One who created fire and who set all things in motion, whose ways were mysterious and whose ends were hidden. He mumbled a prayer that he be forgiven for thinking ill of a man who had always served him well and then set his thoughts back to the road ahead.

At the Brow of Darius, they rejoined the road and followed its winding way over the wind-swept shoulders of the hills, along a narrow gorge where the river raced beside them, a fierce and grumbling companion. Eventually it turned and blocked their path. The only way across was a plank bridge that swayed in the wind stirred by the waters.

Artaban dismounted and led Vasda by the reins but she balked and held back, no matter how hard he tugged. Another man might have cursed his steed for cowardice, quirted her in anger, but Artaban understood her reluctance. He was fearful himself. Still, other men and other mounts had crossed the bridge. They could too. They must!

He spoke softly to her, told her how he counted on her, how he praised her to other men, how much he needed her now. He fed her a dried apple and promised another—the last—once they'd crossed. Reins in hand, he walked ahead and stepped on the bridge and this time she followed behind.

The bridge swayed gently from side to side. Below them, the black waters raged and thundered. He glanced down once and the sight made him queasy. Thereafter he kept his eyes straight ahead, speaking encouragement to Vasda. *"Halfway across now, girl.... Steady, we're doing well.... Just a dozen more steps."*

And then they were over. He laughed with relief and Vasda nuzzled his face. He gave her the promised apple and they were on their way.

By the seventh day they were out of the mountains and passing through a smiling vale with terraces of yellow limestone full of fruit trees. He bought pears and peaches and of course apples from an orchard grower, and he and Vasda gorged themselves on the tender flesh and sweet nectar.

They journeyed on till they came to the stately oak groves of Carine and that which was called the Gates of Zagros, a cleft between two towering cliffs. Seven days of hard riding had taken their toll on Vasda and he walked her the remaining parasangs to Chala, where they would pass the night. It was an ancient city but much reduced by a plague that had swept through a generation before. Many of its houses remained empty and as Artaban rode through the streets at twilight the silence and sight of so many dark windows unnerved him. Had he ridden into the dwelling place of ghosts?

In the silence he heard a loud clacking and when they turned a corner he smiled to see a gang of boys battling each other with wooden swords. A common sight in any other town, hardly worthy of remark, yet here uncommon evidence that falter as it might, life continued.

He found a stable, not what Vasda was used to but it would do for a night. A groom rubbed her down and gave her water and fresh hay. She nibbled a little and then fell asleep. The journey was wearing her more than he expected. He himself was hungry and paid the stable owner to bring a meal from his own table and a blanket to lay on the hay that Artaban might sleep beside his horse.

The next morning he left Chala by the great portal riven in the encircling mountains, passing the image of Zoroaster chiseled in the rock, hand uplifted to bless all wayfarers, both those who worship the One and those who do not, for the life-giving sun shines on everyone, believers and unbelievers alike.

He rode through the valley of the Gyndes, where that peaceful river waters orchards of figs and oranges and grapevines in abundance. The vineyards of the valley were renowned through Persia and beyond. Much he yearned to pass an afternoon under a shady tree with wine and cheese while Vasda munched fallen fruit, but the star beckoned and he pressed on.

The ninth day they spent the morning traversing broad rice fields. He had been walking Vasda—she tired easily since Chala—but Artaban put her into a trot until they were past the fields. Autumnal vapors rose from them, most deadly at night but to be taken lightly at no time.

Now the ground rose and the way wound through a series of shallow hills under shadows of tremulous poplar and tamarind. Once over the hills the road led flat and true as a blade to the bustling city of Seleucia, established by Alexander the Great three hundred years ago. Artaban took a fork that went around it, longer but quicker than pushing their way through the town's crowded, twisty streets.

They camped next to the ruins of a temple to Marduk, Babylon's patron deity. Once pilgrims by the thousand came here to offer sacrifices of lamb or goat, but as that great city had declined from grandeur so did he. Artaban spent a long time brushing the weary Vasda and then ate his dates and bean mash before, weary enough himself, he wrapped himself in his cloak and lay down. The last thing he saw before sleep was the star shining through a thin cloud, beckoning still.

# Chapter Five

## The Dead Man

THE MORNING of the tenth day Vasda was reluctant to rise. He examined her closely for injury or ailment but she suffered from no more than exhaustion. He let her rest for an extra hour but then saddled her. Balthazar and the others would wait for him until tomorrow dawn. If he trotted Vasda most of the way, with breaks for walking, they would make Babylon by evening and the Temple of Fire by midnight. Four Magi would require a small caravan with a retinue to accompany them and among these there would be someone to take his horse back to Babylon and stable her with Ka-mal's cousin.

Late morning they crossed the swirling Tigris on a bridge crowded with traffic: carts of grain and produce, merchant caravans, pilgrims and prostitutes, jostling humanity in all its forms. A little before sunset they reached Babylon, an hour earlier than he expected, which was good because Vasda was tiring fast. He leaned forward and spoke into her ear. "Only a few hours more, girl. Then you've earned a long rest. And a green apple every morning!"

Past Babylon was nothing but peasant huts and stubble-fields. Night fell and he pressed on. Another parasang and by the new moon's dim light he saw the road ahead swallowed in a dark patch. It turned out to be no more than a grove of date palms, but he felt a nameless foreboding as they entered its shadow, the same uneasiness he had in Chala. The place was too quiet and still, no rustle of leaves or cry of night bird.

Vasda too seemed apprehensive, turning her head nervously from side to side. They were almost out of the grove when she whinnied and backed away. Artaban peered into the darkness and saw a figure lying by the side of the road.

He nudged the reluctant Vasda closer. The body was a man's and though it seemed unlikely bait for a bandit trick, he hesitated to dismount. He still had far to go and this one had no claim on him. Yet did not the One command believers to aid travelers in distress?

Still he sat on his mount and pondered. Who was this man and what was he doing here? Perhaps he was hurt or ill. Did he have a horse or camel? Had it wandered? Had he companions and if so, where were they? Perhaps they'd abandoned him. Or perhaps he'd been robbed and left for dead. Perhaps he *was* dead and beyond aid. Then Artaban could ride on with a clear conscience.

At once he was ashamed of this unworthy thought. He was a priest of Zoroaster. If this one was alive, he must be helped. Perhaps he had merely collapsed from exhaustion. In that case, he could be given water and revived.

He dismounted and went to the body, hand on his blade just in case. A moment's inspection told him this was no trap. The man was ill but still alive, though barely. He was a heavy fellow in tattered garments. His skin was pallid and parchment-dry but there was sweat on his brow. Artaban had seen this before: marsh fever, perhaps from a vapor carried by the wind from the rice fields.

He took the man's pulse, faint. His hand was cold and when Artaban let it go, it dropped limply on his breast. This one was only hours from death, likely less than that. Artaban could do little for him. He murmured a prayer for safe passage to the Isle of the Blest and dug in his belt for two half-darics, which he placed on the man's eyelids, payment for burial for whoever found him next. This was right but he also thought it a waste of money. Likely the next traveler would simply pocket the darics and go on, leaving the body to a funeral overseen by kites and desert foxes.

As he rose, the hem of his coat was suddenly clutched by a fleshy hand. Eyelids flickered and the coins slid off. A pair of cloudy, blood-shot eyes stared up at Artaban and a husky voice feebly whispered, *"Help me."*

Artaban looked down. The stranger spoke in Aramaic, the common tongue of this part of Asia, known to Artaban from his travels. He might be any nationality, which made no difference to a priest of Zoroaster, for all people were children of the One.

Yet he was a distraction and an obstacle to one in a great hurry. And truly, what an ill-featured fellow he was! He had a double-chin and bulbous nose, ears large enough to flap in the wind, thick brows and narrow eyes and fat lips and the kind of beard that would not grow or stay shaven, a stubborn stubble that gave him forever an ill-kempt look. From his whisper, Artaban could tell nothing of his voice but he was sure that if the man could say more, he would dislike the sound of him as much as the sight of him.

And just who was this arrogant fellow who carelessly exposed himself to marsh vapors to call on a complete stranger and bid him drop whatever he was doing and care for him like a brother? Who was he to demand Artaban nurse him, soothe him, feed him and so on until he was well or dead? And if dead, no doubt he expected Artaban to pay for a handsome funeral, no hasty half-daric grave! Likely he was also expected to carry the sad news to the wretch's miserable parents in Damascus or wherever, perhaps to marry his equally ill-featured sister to boot. Really, what presumption!

"Help..." the man croaked again, his eyes falling shut.

Artaban sighed. There was little he could do. Yet that little he must do at least. No follower of the One should do less, certainly no priest of Zoroaster. *Well, fellow,* thought Artaban. *I will give you water and a blanket to make easy your dying, but there your dubious claim on me ends.* He bent and slipped his arms under the body and lifted him, carrying him—*truly, a heavy one!*—to a little mound under a date palm.

He undid the man's turban and loosened his robe. Then he went to Vasda, slumped wearily by the side of the road and doubtless glad of the delay, and from the saddlebags took his pouch of healing powders. *Well,* he thought, *I can mix a plaster in a few minutes. He's a little farther from death than I thought. With this he might last through the night. If I leave him the coins, he might buy aid from the next traveler.*

He moistened the sick one's lips with water and then knelt beside him and mixed a paste of ground mustard seed and ginger and coarse flour. This he spread on the man's heaving chest. After a little the fellow's eyelids flickered again. Artaban gave him more water and this time he was able to sip from the skin. He opened his eyes and his hand weakly brushed at his chest. *"Hot,"* he murmured in Aramaic, the common language for most of the region east of Babylon.

"Yes, hot," said Artaban in the same tongue. "You have a chill in your lungs. The heat will drive it away... I hope. But your head is hotter, a fever. In a minute I'll give you something that will cool you there. Balance is the key to health. Right now your body is out of balance. If I can get your hot parts cooler and your cold parts warmer, you might pull through."

The man stared at him blankly, uncomprehending, then his eyes closed. Artaban built a fire, poured a little water in a small bowl and added various powders. He stirred them and heated the potion. He waited till it bubbled, then put it aside till it cooled. He helped his patient to a sitting position and held it to his lips. By now the man was able to hold the bowl himself.

"It's bitter," Artaban cautioned, "but don't spit it out. Swallow. It's for your fever."

The man made a face at the taste but he drank it all. He lay back on his blanket but this time his eyes stayed open. "Are you a physician?" he rasped.

"It's not my profession," Artaban replied, "but I know physick. I'm a priest of Zoroaster."

"Are you going to leach me?"

"No."

"Bless you. I hate leaches."

"Leaches do no good and sometimes much harm. There's no such thing as bad blood. To draw it doesn't draw out illness, it weakens the patient."

He was about to explain further but the man had fallen asleep. He judged that his patient had improved to the point where his chances of living or dying were about equal. The next hour or so would tell.

He unsaddled and brushed Vasda, then took out his glass and studied the stars. An hour passed without change but an hour after that, the man rolled on his side and began to spit up a vile-smelling green fluid. This went on for several minutes, then he lay on the blanket, exhausted. Artaban wiped his patient's mouth and smiled. The worst was over.

He poured water in a small pot, added dried leaves and heated it over the fire. He replaced his powders in the pouch and packed the pouch in the saddlebags. He saddled Vasda and went back to the fire, where he removed the pot. He poured some tea in a bowl and offered it to the man, who was sitting up and watching him.

"Drink the whole pot," Artaban said. "By morning, you'll be able to stand and walk a little. Rest for a day. After that, you should be yourself."

The man sipped the tea. "I'm hungry," he said.

"Good. Here's dried fruit and bean mash. I'd offer you better but that's all I have. Did you come on a mount?"

"No. I travel on foot."

"Have you money?"

"A little."

Artaban gave him the two half-darics. "These were to pay for your burial. Now they'll buy you food and maybe a ride in a cart."

"What is your name, friend?"

"Artaban."

"I'm called Ismail. Where are you bound?"

"I have friends waiting for me in Borsippa."

"Fellow Magi?"

"Yes! How did you know?"

"I come from Akkad. I met them on the road. We traveled together for a while. Myself, I'm a man of no education but I admire learning. You and they are seeking a child born under the new star."

"Yes. We go to Jerusalem."

"They said as much, to talk to scholars. My people have prophecies of such a one, the messiah, we call him."

"You're Jewish?"

"Half of me is, though I couldn't tell you which half. My mother, may she rest in peace, was a Jew. I travel too much to keep to any faith, so I just worship whoever the locals do. I see you've saddled. Must you leave?"

"My friends depart at dawn. I have to go if I'm to join them."

"Then go with the One, priest of Zoroaster. And with Jehovah. And with any other god who'll speed you on your way." He burst into tears.

Artaban put his hand on Ismail's arm. "What's the matter?"

"Nothing," said Ismail, snuffling with embarrassment. "Nothing at all. Forgive me. I'm an emotional man, my mother's side, you know. I'm just... overcome at your kindness and goodness." Tears spouted from his eyes. "You don't know me, owe me nothing, yet you saved my life!" He grabbed Artaban's wrist with his other hand and pulled him close. "Let me embrace you!"

Artaban endured this for a moment. He was glad for Ismail's gratitude but the sick man was dirty from days on the road and smelled of vomit. When Artaban tried to pull away, the other held him even tighter and would not let go. He wriggled and squirmed and finally managed to pry an arm loose, then the second arm, only to find the first arm was around him again. All the while Ismail flooded him with tears, bawling like a newborn.

"Thank you, my friend," gasped Artaban, squeezed in Ismail's tight embrace. "Many thanks, but I have to go."

"My friend, my rescuer, blessed holy man!" cried Ismail, eyes wet with gratitude, nose dribbling with something less agreeable. His arms held Artaban tight and his hands roved like a lover's. There seemed no part of the Mage's person that he did not want to touch in thanks.

At length Artaban pulled free. He scrambled away from Ismail's grasp and backed toward Vasda. "Be well, friend," he said, hand on his blade in case Ismail rose to embrace him again.

But he did not. "Godspeed, Artaban, greatest of Magi!" he cried. "Find your friends! Follow your star!

Blessed art thou among healers and holy men. May Heaven watch over you!"

Artaban leaped onto Vasda and spurred her away. Racing out of the palm grove and into the pale light of the setting moon, he heard Ismail calling thanks and blessings until he was far down the road.

# Chapter Six

## The Temple of Fire

IT WAS later than he'd realized. There were scant hours to dawn. The moon was nearly down and the stars cast little light. The road could be hardly seen but he spurred Vasda on in full gallop. The mare was tired, more than tired, and when his spurs could not prod her to greater speed, he reluctantly used his quirt.

"Forgive me, girl," he said. "Only a little further. We must make Borsippa by first light!"

She stretched her legs and shot ahead. Even in the dark, with only shadows for landmarks, he knew she was running as she never had, spending her all for him. The wind stung his cheeks. "On, girl! Faster!" he urged.

Overhead, the star beckoned as they hurtled toward Borsippa. Now all Artaban's senses were confined to his place atop his horse. The moon was gone and in the enfolding blackness that hid even Vasda's head, he was blind, the star all he could see. The heavy scent of his sweat and Vasda's was all he could smell. The rocking of himself in the saddle was all he felt, the loud thunder of her hooves all he heard. Never had he known such speed! He half-imagined they had left the road and taken to the air, soaring above the clouds, galloping across the vast vault of sky. All that existed now was himself, his mount, the inky night and the cold light of a lantern that never grew nearer.

But the star began to fade. A strip of blackness became deep purple as the horizon revealed itself. The underside of clouds glowed red with the heat of the rising sun and the sky paled. The road before them grew gray and then brown. Shadows of houses rushed past. They had reached the outskirts of Borsippa, but the Temple of Fire was on the other side of town.

They had come as far as the marketplace when Vasda collapsed with exhaustion, sinking to her knees. Artaban leaped off and tugged at her reins. "Up, girl! Up!" He beseeched, he begged, he cajoled. "Half a parasang more. That's all! Then you may rest, long as you like. And all the apples you want!"

She struggled to her feet and he leaped on top. She galloped on, her breath coming in short, pained wheezes. Now it was broad daylight and people were about. They stopped and stared at the rider galloping through their town on the frothing steed. The two hurtled through the narrow streets and the houses grew fewer. Now they had passed Borsippa. Far ahead, he could see the Temple of Fire, its dome gleaming in the morning sun.

They overtook a pair of lumbering carts, hauled by oxen and taking up the entire road. Artaban steered Vasda around them, barely breaking stride, and now the Temple was close, its interior glowing with the ever-lit fire within. Worshippers milled around it. He saw several men leading camels.

"Balthazar!" he called at the distant figures. "I'm here! Here at last! Caspar! Melchior! Friends, bless you for waiting! I'm—"

With a loud whinny, Vasda collapsed again. This time her knees buckled and she fell on her side. Artaban leaped free just in time to escape a crushed leg. "Sweet Vasda," he cried. "You've done it! We're here!" He left her and ran to the temple. Worshippers watched him approach with confusion and some apprehension. Who was this fellow? What was his hurry? What was he about? Was he in his right mind?

Artaban scanned the curious faces. At sight of the camels, he ran to greet his friends. "Balthazar, Melchior—"

But the men with camels were strangers. "I'm looking for three priests," he told them. "They're waiting for me. Where are they? Do you know?"

They shook their heads dumbly. He turned to others leaving the temple. "I seek three Magi," he said, tapping shoulders and tugging at sleeves. "Friends of mine, have you seen them? They're here somewhere."

He met shrugs and incomprehension and now and then annoyed looks. Three Magi? No one had seen them. No one had any idea where they might be. No one knew what he was talking about.

*Perhaps they've been delayed,* thought Artaban. Something must have happened on the road and they had not arrived yet. He was early! Of all things, early!

"They're gone," said a voice. Artaban turned. The speaker wore a winged circle like himself and the vestments of the temple priest. "You seek Balthazar and the others?"

"Yes. What do you mean they've gone."

"I mean they've gone on. They left well before day, two hours ago. You are Artaban?"

"I am. Did they leave a message, any word for me?"

"Only to follow. Balthazar said to tell you they were bound for Jerusalem."

"Did they leave me a camel?"

"They planned to, but one of theirs took lame and they couldn't spare any. There are camels to be had in Babylon."

"I suppose there are," mumbled Artaban. He thanked the temple priest and walked away. Gone! They hadn't waited. Lofty, impatient men! What would it have cost them to stay another hour or two? Had he not divined the meaning of the star as much as they? More! They'd still be stuck on their stools in dusty library nooks were it not for him! He wouldn't be surprised if they got lost in the desert, wandering in circles until the star was gone. They'd arrive in Jerusalem years late. *We have gifts for the babe.* *Oh, the babe? He's all grown up, has babes of his own now. You're welcome to give your gifts to them.* Arrogant fools!

Vasda was laying where he left her, legs spread, head on the ground. "Brave girl!" he said as he approached. "No more running for you! Rest until you can walk. Then we'll go into town and I'll find you a stable."

But she lifted not her head and as he knelt, he saw blood had pooled from her nostrils. Her flanks were still and her eyes stared blankly. With a gasp, he saw that Vasda, valiant Vasda, fleetest of the horses in Persia; worth more than rubies and sapphires and pearls; beloved by her master; she who would let none but him on her back; she full of grace and beauty and vain as a princess; she great of heart; she, Vasda, his dearest possession, was lifeless and dead.

Those passing on the road saw a sight not unknown to them, a fallen horse. It was common enough. Horses died, sometimes on the road. It was a nuisance and an inconvenience and a hazard to health for it attracted birds of prey and contagions grew from the body. A dead horse was no strange sight then. What was strange was the sight of a man, surely its owner, his hands around its neck, weeping like one who'd lost a wife or child. Moreover, he was begging forgiveness from this dead creature for some crime or misdeed. A crime against whom? A crime against a horse? Surely not. One can steal a horse. That is a crime, but against its owner, not the horse. One can't steal from a horse. After all, what has a horse to steal?

AT LENGTH, Artaban collected himself. He gathered his saddlebags and found some boys who found some men who would haul away his horse and bury her. As payment, he told them they might have her saddle, which they could sell for enough to buy a small herd of horses. He gave the oldest man a half daric to be sure it was properly done. "I want her buried, do you understand?"

"Yes sir."

"Buried deep. Do not leave her for the kites. Do you understand?"

"I do."

"And pile a cairn over her."

"As you wish."

"As you are a man of honor, will you do this for me?"

"I will do it. You have paid handsomely but as a man of honor, I would do it for less. Shall I come to you when it is done and tell you where she rests?"

"No, for you bury her body, not her. Her resting place is in my heart. Now stand off a little."

"As you wish, sir."

The men walked away a distance and Artaban knelt beside Vasda. He stroked her mane and spoke softly, as one would lullaby a child. "So the One took a handful of south wind and another of running water and molded them, saying, 'I create thee, O Arabian. To thy forelock, I bind victory in battle and upon thy back I heap its spoils. To thy loins I confer might and fury, and to thy legs speed like no other. Much am I pleased with thee, for thou art one of the glories of this earth. Let all gaze...'"

He stopped for a moment, unable to continue. After a moment, he bent and kissed her forelock and continued, "'Let all gaze and marvel, for I give thee flight without wings!'"

And then he stood and walked away and he did not look back.

# Chapter Seven

## The Dying Man

A PENNY bought Artaban a ride on a cart into Borsippa. The cart was half full of produce and the other half was occupied by wayfarers. He was not used to traveling by foot or sharing a cart with common people and he found their company irksome. They smelled and jabbered of small things: daily matters, gossip, their aches and pains and how to cure them, which mostly consisted of spells and prayers to their favorite gods.

But what did he expect from cart riders? They were lowly people with small lives and small thoughts. They were superstitious and full of folly and their world was low-roofed and narrow. They spent the day chattering and bickering and at night they saw the stars and neither wondered nor understood.

The cart trundled on. A small boy, very small, beat the side of the cart with a stick repeatedly and Artaban yearned to yank it from him and hurl it away – or perhaps hurl away both stick and urchin. The irritation must have shown on his face for at length the boy noticed his gaze and, frightened, dropped the stick and pressed against his mother, bawling. She comforted him and looked darkly at Artaban, who turned away.

*These are unworthy thoughts,* he said to himself. This woman loved her child as much as any mother whose husband could buy her a perch on a camel. These people were unlettered but they weren't fools. Their world was small but not because they did not long for something larger. They knew sorrow and bore it, and he must do the same. *My master taught that a vine watered with tears bears bitter fruit. In a few days I will join my brothers and when I do, I must bring a glad heart and joy at the good tidings brought by the star.*

Then he turned and gave a half-daric to the surprised mother and smiled at the boy, who, uncomprehending, burst into tears again.

In Borsippa, Artaban left the cart and walked to an inn recommended by the carter. The walk was not long but he found himself tired and by the time he reached the door felt weak and faint. He paid for a private room and slowly followed the innkeeper's daughter upstairs.

The room was little more than a table with water pitcher, a chamber pot and a low bed with a corn husk mattress. The girl told him she would bring him candles when night fell. That was also when supper was served, though she could bring his own upstairs if he wished. She pointed to the bolt on the door and said that her father's was the only inn between here and Babylon to provide guests such security, so though he might pay a little more, he would sleep without worry.

She was a chatty girl and might have gone on to explain the superior quality of the bed and even the chamber pot, but Artaban gave her a penny and told her to bring his supper when she brought the candles. When she left, he bolted the door and removed his robe and money belt and lay down, uncommonly tired.

He woke at loud knocking and staggered to the door to let in the girl. He told her to light the candles but take back the food as he had no appetite. As she was about to leave, he said to ask her mother to call on him. When she was gone he collapsed on his bed. *I have marsh fever.*

When the innkeeper's wife came, he told her he was a physician and ill with an ailment that he'd had before, that it was not catching and he would be well in a few days if she followed his instructions. He would of course pay for her trouble.

The woman, whose name was Rachel, was a plump, kindly soul and said she would do all she could. He directed her to his saddlebags and told her what she needed from it and how to make a healing paste.

She left and came back with it shortly. He told her to he would apply it himself, as only he knew how. Then he told her what herbs to take from his bag to make a healing tea. She must make a pot tonight and another in the morning. He might be well on the morrow but if not, then likely on the day after. Aside from herself, no one should come in his room as he needed absolute quiet, and when she came she should leave the tea by his bed and go. If he was asleep, she should make a noise but not touch him on any account, as his illness made his skin very sensitive and touch was painful.

She left to make the tea and he applied the paste to his chest, thinking, *I do not care to hide the truth but if I am thrown into the street I will surely die. So long as this woman does not come close, she should be safe enough.*

61

*Now by the will of the One, I will either live or die. If I live, I will join my fellow Magi and fulfill my quest and return to Rasha and never leave my home again. If I die, I will be buried without ceremony and my grave forgotten. That would be hard but all that happens is the will of the One, who sets all things in motion.*

The innkeeper's wife returned with the mustard paste. Artaban thanked her and asked that she bring pen and ink and three pieces of parchment. She said that they had pen and ink but no parchment. There was, however, a holy man who could read and write and he had parchment. She could bring them tomorrow. Artaban replied that he must have it tonight and said he would pay ten pennies to her and ten to the holy man.

She told him she would send her son, then left to make his tea. He forced himself to stay awake until she returned. Some time later, he was on his second cup of tea when she reappeared with pen and ink and parchment. He thanked her and said she need not come back till morning.

When she was gone, he took the first parchment and by the flickering candlelight wrote:

*Worthy Jabar, greetings to you. I am in Borsippa, ill with swamp fever. If you receive this letter, know that I have died of it. It grieves me to tell you that Vasda is also dead. She died serving me to her last heartbeat. Dispose of my goods, including my house, and with the proceeds pay twelve years wages to yourself and a year's wages to all but Ka-mal and Fashid. Pay Ka-mal three years wages and give him all the horses in my stable. As to Fashid, I wish him to go to Bagdad to attend the school of Harouk the Teacher until his eighteenth year. Decide what this will cost and set aside the money, which I wish you to administer. He should return once a year to visit his parents and also to report to you what he has learned and what he intends to do with his learning. Give him such advice as you think proper. You have a way with boys and I think with guidance Fashid will become a worthy man. What remains of my money, give to the temple priest for distribution to the poor. Give him also all my scrolls. You know, I am sure, that you are more than a faithful servant to me. I shall miss you and we shall both miss the sound of my house ringing again with childish laughter and a woman's song. This is hard but it is the will of the One, who sets all things in motion and ends all our days.*

*Artaban*

When he had written this, he took a second parchment and wrote:

*Worthy Tigranes, greetings to you. I am in Borsippa, ill with swamp fever. If you receive this letter, know that I have died of it and therefore your daughter is free to marry another. This is the will of the One, who sets all in motion and ends all our days. I have written a letter also to her, which I ask that you pass on if you deem it proper.*

He put away the parchment and drank a cup of the tea prepared for him and wiped the sweat from his forehead with a rag. He picked up the third parchment but did not write, staring at it for a long while. Finally he wrote:

*Beloved Rasha, it grieves me to write these words, knowing that you will not read them unless I am no more. Your father, I am sure, has already told you of this and soon there will be other suitors at his door, seeking your hand in marriage. All this is as it should be. I hope that you will find a worthy husband and the two of you have many children. I admit this hope is tempered with sorrow, since your chil-*

*dren will not be my children. I am many years older than you and fully expected to take leave of life before you, but I had hoped it would not be until my beard had grown truly grey, and that I drew my last breath in the arms of she whom I love as I have no other. Farewell.*

When he was done, he put the parchments away. The effort of composing the three letters had exhausted him and he gratefully lay his head on the pillow, asleep within moments.

# Chapter Eight

## Robbed!

THE NEXT morning his forehead was still hot and the chill in his chest had taken cold hold of him. He had the innkeeper's wife prepare another mustard plaster and then told her to send someone to ask the priest of the Temple of Fire to visit a fellow priest whose own fire was low.

The temple priest, whose name was Musa, came late the same day. Upon sight of Artaban, he said, "You are the one who sought the three bound for Jerusalem. I am sorry to see you ill." He did not ask what was wrong but he stood away from the bed and did not come closer.

"I am yet hopeful I will rise, but I may not," said Artaban. "If I should die, I have three letters I wish delivered to Ecbatana. I can pay for this. Will you see it done?"

"For a brother of the Way, I would see it done without payment."

"I am glad to hear it but I will pay anyway. One letter goes to Jabar of the house of Artaban the Mage. The two others go to the merchant Tigranes and his daughter."

The priest took the parchments. "I will keep this until I hear from you or hear news of your death. If it needs be done, I will see it done."

"Blessings on you, worthy one. Now on another matter, if you lift my cloak, you will find my money belt. In it are five pockets. The first two contain darics and half-darics. The next two are filled with pennies. Leave the pennies but take the darics and half-darics for safe-keeping. If I recover, I will claim them. If I do not, use some to pay for my burial and the rest in the name of Zoroaster as you see fit."

The priest took the money and put it in his pouch. "If it must be done, I will see it done. And I will say a prayer for you at temple that all may know your gift."

"Thank you. Now in the fifth pocket is a small purse. In the purse is—"

"There is no purse."

"There is. It is a small purse. Look again."

"There is no purse."

"What do you mean there is no purse?"

"I mean there is no purse. See for yourself." He handed the belt to Artaban, who sat up and stared at the empty pocket. He put his finger inside and probed but the priest spoke true. There was no purse. His jewels were gone!

Artaban examined each of the belt's pockets and finally tossed it on the floor. "I had gifts," he said. "Three gifts for him born under the star."

"I am sorry to hear this."

"A ruby, a sapphire and a pearl. Priceless."

"They must have been stolen."

"Not by the people who keep this inn. I cannot believe it of them."

"Did you bolt your door last night?"

"No. I fell asleep."

"Then anyone could have slipped in."

"Why not take a handful of darics and slip out? No one knew about my gifts. How could they know what was most precious?"

"You had spoken of them to no one?"

"No one."

"Did you stop on your way at a tavern? Talk with strangers?"

"I spent one night at an inn and another in a stable. At the inn I stayed in my room. At neither place did I speak of my gifts."

"Did you have a drink with anyone?"

"No. I seldom drink and not at all on this trip."

"From time to time, did you take out the jewels to admire?"

"No. I haven't looked at them since Ecbatana."

"Then they could have been stolen on the road."

"I don't see how."

"Nor do I but however it happened they are gone now. I am sorry for this and would help you if I could but I can't. In any case I have duties back at the temple."

They said farewell and the priest left. Artaban lay on his bed. Gone! His gifts for the child were gone and he had no hope of getting them back. He couldn't afford to buy three more such jewels, not even one more. Even if he could, the delay would keep him from catching up with Balthazar and the others.

Only twelve days before, he had set out with high hopes on the finest horse in Persia with priceless gifts for a babe born to rule. His quest was great and great glory lay before him as among the first to honor the child who would be king. Now his hopes were dashed, his horse dead, his gifts stolen. Perhaps it was better he die here among strangers than return home diminished and defeated.

He fell into a troubled sleep. Had the Shadow come into his room and beckoned, he would have put up little resistance. But the will of the One is hidden and so it happened that he awoke and was barely able to grab the chamber pot before he threw up green gobs of vomit. Afterwards, he lay on the bed and touched his forehead, which was cool. His fever had broken. His misery was just as great but he knew he must somehow bear it for he was going to live.

TWO DAYS later, Artaban sat on a bench at a table in the inn's common room, dipping a spoon into a thin broth made for him by the good-hearted innkeeper's wife. His spirits were low and he was in no mood to be with people but neither was he in a mood to stay in his room and ponder the spider who had begun to build a web in the corner.

Tomorrow he would leave on a donkey for Babylon, there to buy a mount to take him home. The temple priest had returned his letters and coins and the darics were back in his money belt, which he was wearing. He was not unhappy to be leaving Borsippa but neither did he look forward to the trip back. He knew his failure would make no difference to Rasha or her father or to his household, but it did to him. It crushed him. He had gone off to do a great thing and he had not done it. He would have done better to stay on his roof and gaze through his glass at the stars. He would at least not have thrown away his money on jewels that doubtless were now adorning some thief's harlot.

He sipped a spoonful of broth. It was plain but hot and nourishing and though he had little appetite, he was glad for what little he had. He must regain his strength. He was about to swallow another spoonful when a hand clapped him on the back. "Mage! Beloved Mage!" said a voice. Someone plopped on the bench next to him and wrapped an arm around his shoulder. "Healer! Miracle worker! Samaritan! What fortune to bump into you!"

Artaban turned to see who addressed him so companionably. Bulbous nose, double-chin, great flaps of ears, thick brows, narrow eyes, beard that would not grow or stay shaven. Truly, who could forget such a constellation of homely features? This could be no other than…

"Ismail!" said the one beside him. "I am Ismail, worthy Artaban." He wrapped both hands around Artaban and hugged him tightly. "He whom you saved from death on the road to Borsippa. Don't you remember?"

"How could I forget? I'm glad to see you alive and well."

"No gladder than I am!" laughed the other heartily. "Let me embrace you, rescuer!" Before Artaban could protest he had been enveloped in a two-armed hug, Ismail's hands roving over his body as before, restlessly squeezing and rubbing and patting his flesh like a customer at a fruit stall.

At length Artaban broke free. "Enough! Enough, Ismail. Do you embrace everyone this way?"

"Only those who've saved my life!" laughed Ismail, spreading his arms. Before he could grab his rescuer again, however, Artaban moved to the bench across the table. He slid his soup after him. "Stay if you wish, but stay where you are," he told Ismail. "I'm in no mood for embraces."

"Are you all right?" asked Ismail with concern. "You look pale."

"I was ill."

Ismail's face clouded. "Ill? With what?"

"We won't speak of what, not here in an inn full of people."

"But you're all right now?" Ismail said anxiously. "You are! I can tell you are."

"I instructed the innkeeper's wife on what to do. It was a close thing."

Ismail's eyes filled with tears. He grabbed Artaban's hand, pulled it across the table and kissed it. "Dearest friend. I should never forgive myself had you..."

With difficulty Artaban pulled the hand away. Still tearful, Ismail rose to come around and embrace him. No weapon handy, Artaban thrust the spoon at him. "No more embracing! Sit back down."

Ismail reluctantly sat. "But you're all right?" he asked again.

"I'm all right now. Put yourself at peace. I did what for you I did knowing the risks. Enough of this. Tell me what you are doing here."

"I was on my way to Babylon when you found me. I've done my business there and now I'm on my way back. I came here for a bite and a bed and, well, here you are! What fortune!"

"Your business must have been profitable. You hadn't inn-money when I saw you last."

"I can't complain, can't complain. But what about you? Why aren't you with your fellow Magi bound for Jerusalem?"

"I missed them by two hours. I'm bound for home."

"But why is this, my friend? I wouldn't think you're a man who quits when he stumbles."

"I have reasons," Artaban replied. A vague but terrible suspicion was forming in his mind. Ismail had traded his tattered garments for a robe suitable for a rising merchant. Instead of a dirty cloth turban, he wore one of silk adorned with a small feather. He no longer smelled foul. In fact he smelled sweet, too much so, like one who'd soaked in a scented bath or been rubbed with a honeyed ointment. Where came the coin for these embellishments? What was his business in Babylon? Artaban took a spoonful of broth. "I have my reasons," he repeated.

"Doubtless you do," murmured Ismail tactfully.

"You see," Artaban went on in a conversational way. "I had gifts for the one born under the star."

"Yes, your friends had gifts too. Balthazar's was gold and Melchior's frank—"

"Whatever they had, my gifts *beggared* theirs."

"Doubtless, doubtless."

"I had a ruby, bright as the rising sun," Artaban said, careful to keep his voice level.

"Sounds beautiful."

"And a sapphire, blue as a bay in the morning light."

"Ah, exquisite."

"And dearest of all, a perfect pearl, fit for a sea god."

"Magnificent!"

"But they were stolen from me."

Ismail's eyebrows leaped and his eyes grew wide with alarm. "What? Stolen? How? When?"

"Somewhere on the road. I kept them in a small purse, tucked away in a pocket of a money belt I wore under my robe."

"Very shrewd. You can't be too careful on the road."

"Clearly I wasn't careful enough. Someone took the purse from my belt."

"When? You don't mean…" Ismail glanced at the innkeeper and his bustling wife. "They seem such honest people."

"No, I was robbed before Borsippa. I've narrowed it down to a certain stretch of road, one you've been on yourself."

"Is that so? But perhaps you *weren't* robbed."

"Of course I was robbed!"

"Perhaps you merely overlooked your purse. You had a fever, right? It could happen."

"Impossible. It's gone. And I think I know—"

"Have you checked?"

"What do you mean, have I checked?"

"I mean lately. Have you looked lately?"

"The purse is gone!"

"Perhaps not."

Artaban was baffled. Ismail seemed utterly serious. "I don't know what you're up to," Artaban told him, "but it won't—"

"Dear friend, just check. I beg you!"

Without taking his eyes off the other, Artaban reached under his robe. His hand slipped along the pockets of his belt. First pocket, darics. Second pocket, half-darics. Third and fourth pockets, pennies. Fifth pocket, empty. No, wait. Not empty! It felt like...

Artaban took his hand from his robe. In it he held the missing purse. He opened it. Inside were the sapphire and pearl.

He looked up. Ismail sat staring at him, all innocent interest. Artaban lunged across the table, knocking over his soup, and seized Ismail by the throat. *"WHERE'S THE RUBY?"* he roared.

Ismail clutched at Artaban's wrist, trying to pull his hand off, but the thief was held in an unbreakable grip.

"I..." gasped Ismail. "please... can't..."

Artaban glanced around. Every eye in the inn was on the two of them. More talk of jewels here wasn't wise. He let go of Ismail's neck and grabbed him by the collar of his robe. He stood pulling the other to his feet. "Outside," he said tersely. "If you try to run, I'll—"

"I haven't come back to run away," Ismail said with an effort at dignity, massaging his neck as Artaban dragged him through the door and into the street.

Outside the inn, Artaban pushed him against a wall. "Why *have* you come back?" he demanded. "Where's my ruby?"

"One question at a time. I'm back because of my mother, may she rest in peace. As to the ruby, I lost it in Babylon, in a game of bones."

Artaban's hands flew around Ismail's neck again. "You *gambled* away my ruby?"

"The fellow had a diamond the equal of the ruby. I did you a great wrong and I thought to make amends by returning your jewels and making a gift of the diamond."

Artaban clouted Ismail on the ear. "You're lying!"

"*Owww!* All right, perhaps I wanted the diamond for myself," squeaked Ismail, straining his neck against Artaban's grasp. "I've always been lucky with the bones. *Owww!* Don't hit me. I'm telling the truth. I swear on my mother's grave."

"You really lost the ruby? You're not holding it back?"

"No, I swear. If I had it and held it back, she'd never give me peace."

"Who?"

"My mother."

"You just said she was dead."

"Yes and no. Let me tell my story, all of it. And please let go of my neck. I can barely breath, much less talk. When I'm done, if you still want, you can clout me all you like."

"I'll do that and worse," said Artaban, loosening his grip. "Tell it then."

"As you've divined, I took the purse from your belt. A sin, surely, but a man must live and that's how I make my living."

"How did you know there were jewels in the purse?"'

"I didn't but the purse felt empty. I doubted you'd hidden an empty purse in your belt so whatever was inside had to be very small. What's small and precious? It was a guess based on experience. I've been inside money belts before."

Artaban let go of Ismail and sank onto a nearby bench. Gone, his ruby was truly gone! " How could you rob the man who saved your life?"

"The very question my mother asked my first night in Babylon. You see, after you left, I drank your tea and come morning I could stand and walk around. By then there was traffic on the road and with your money I paid for a ride on a cart. Once in Babylon, I went to the shop of a rug dealer who'd bought goods from me before. He wasn't in but his son said he would be the next day. With nothing to do, I went to a tavern where I knew there was always a game of bones going on in back. As I said, I'm lucky with them. I used the rest of your money as stakes and three hours later I'd won a handsome sum. Just as I was about to leave the man with the diamond ring joined us. It was as handsome a stone as I've seen and I made the mistake of thinking I couldn't lose, so the two of us tossed the bones for our jewels."

"You're not just a thief. You're a fool."

"A fool I was but I learned from my folly and left the game while I was ahead. I went to the town's best inn and bought a room and a meal. I went to sleep feeling pleased with myself but in the middle of the night, my mother came to me, wearing an apron with flour on her hands just as in life. 'Ismail,' she told me, 'you've done many bad things in your life. Yet you were a good son to me and I've always loved you. But this, this I cannot ignore! You were brought back from the dead by a good and kindly man, a priest of Zoroaster. And you repaid him by stealing his gems! You must find him and give back the two you still have. Promise me you'll do that! I can't rest in my grave until you've done so.' And then she began to wail, tears streaming down her round cheeks. She wailed and wailed. I woke up in a cold sweat. She's been back every night since. I haven't had a full night's sleep in a week."

"I'm touched by your plight," said Artaban with a mirthless smile. "So it wasn't good fortune that you found me here."

"No, though it's good fortune that I'm not on a camel on the road to Judea right now. I went to the Temple of Fire, thinking maybe the priest could tell me something more about you and the others. That's when I learned you were here, recovering from an illness. So that's my story. Enough of what's past. Let us speak of what's to come. When do we leave, Master?"

"I'm not your Master," said Artaban, rising from the bench. "And 'we' are not going anywhere. You've made your amends, such as they are. Now get out of my sight." He went back inside the inn.

"Two stones is not three stones," said Ismail, following him inside. "But they're still worthy gifts, as fine or finer than anything your friends have."

Artaban sat at his table and lifting the spoon to his porridge. "If they spent time in your company, "I'm surprised they still have the clothes on their backs. Don't sit down. If you do, I'll have the innkeeper throw you out."

Ismail didn't sit but neither did he leave. "Master, I don't rob everyone I meet."

"Stop calling me 'Master," said Artaban. He made a face. The porridge was cold. "I'm going to Jerusalem, but without you." He gestured to the serving girl and told her to bring him a fresh bowl.

"First you have to go to Babylon to buy camels and provisions," said Ismail. "You'll need a guide too. You have a desert to cross and it's easy to get lost. You'll lose precious days when you could be on the road with me. I've been to Judea many times and know the way exceeding well."

The girl set a hot bowl of porridge in front of Artaban. "Why are you so bound to come with me? You've done what you can to right your wrong. Your mother can rest in her grave." He swallowed a spoonful. Well, at least it was hot.

"I told her I'd see to it you got your gifts to this child. I lost your ruby, yes, but I had the money I won. Don't you want to know what I did with it?"

Artaban forced himself to swallow another spoon. "Bought yourself new clothes and an ointment that smells like a harlot's bedroom."

"That and four camels and provisions for two. They're in a stable just a ten minute walk from here. I'm your slave until we find the babe. I promised Mama."

Not a little stunned, Artaban put down his spoon and turned to stare at Ismail. Was the man mad? Was he jesting? The thief stood before him, hands clasped humbly together, the very picture of devoted service. He seemed gifted at picking up a role and playing it as though born to the position. Artaban had no doubt that if he were posing as an innkeeper he would be the perfect innkeeper. If a priest, the perfect priest. If a pimp, the perfect pimp.

Ismail was about to speak again but Artaban waved him into silence. He sat there for long minutes, lost in thought. After a while he opened the purse in his hand and emptied the contents into his palm. The sapphire gleamed brightly. The pearl shone with creamy luster. He carefully put them back in the purse and looked at Ismail. "Four camels?"

"Yes and fine beasts too, the best on the market. Their names are Gypsy, Hannah, Champion and Little Bit." Without asking, he picked up Artaban's spoon and dipped into the porridge."

"What about provisions?"

Ismail swallowed the porridge and made a face. "Tasteless gruel. Too much salt, no cinnamon and made with water instead of milk. I make a morning porridge that will warm you and fill you. As to provisions, I bought dates, olives, dried beans, dried goat, meal for mornings, salt, cinnamon and much else. I'm a fine cook, learned it from Mama. I also bought a tent. I can put it up in ten minutes. I'll get the water, set up camp, load and unload the camels. Whatever you need, consider it done by your faithful slave."

"I don't want a slave. I don't believe any man should own another."

"As you say, Master."

"And if I did believe that, you are the last person on earth I would want to own."

"Of course, Master."

"But you may serve me until we find the babe. I will pay you a half-daric each week."

"Master, you needn't pay me any—"

"Yes, I do. You are a free man who serves me, not a slave. Servants are paid, slaves not."

"Very well, Master."

"Two things are forbidden to you while in my service. No gambling and no thieving."

"As you say, Master."

"And the moment I give my gifts, our contract is done. We go our separate ways. May it please the One, I hope to never see you again. Until then, we travel together."

"I want nothing else, Master, " said Ismail, tears of gratitude welling in his eyes. He dropped to his knees and grabbed Artaban's hand to kiss it but his new master yanked it away and clouted him on the ear with a promise to do worse if his new servant embraced him again.

# Chapter Nine

## Herod

THE NEXT morning the two set out. They stopped at the Temple of Fire and Artaban thanked the priest there for his help, who said that he was glad to see Artaban fully recovered and glad too that his friend had found him.

"He's my servant, not my friend," Artaban replied crisply. He bade the other farewell and the two embraced. Artaban mounted his camel and the small caravan plodded off. The temple priest watched them until they were only tiny shapes on the horizon. *May the One watch over you*, he silently prayed. *For that way lies a hard journey.*


HIGH on the backs of their camels, the Mage and his servant passed over the dreary undulations of the desert, rocking steadily like ships on the waves. By day the air quivered with the heat, no creatures but themselves on the swooning earth except lizards and jerboas—desert rodents with oversized ears scuttling through the parched brush. At night, the fever of the day was followed by a bitter, blighting cold.

The shifting hills of sand eventually gave way to a flat, featureless country broken only by dark ledges of rocks that thrust themselves through the ground like the bones of perished monsters. Good it was that they were fully provisioned, for the stony wastes bore no fruit but briars and thorns. The ground rose and they passed over a low mountain range, furrowed with dry channels cut by ancient torrents, white as scars on the face of nature. At night they heard jackals barking and once the ravines echoed with a lion's loud roar.

So through heat and cold, the star beckoned them on through the trackless wastes. At length they reached Damascus, with its plentiful gardens and orchards, green swards sloping from its rivers adorned with blooms and fragrant clusters of roses and myrrh. From there they followed a narrow path through the cedars that rose from the long snowy ridge of Hermon and then through the valley of the Jordan to the blue waters of the Lake of Galilee.

The tenth day of their journey they reached the walls of Jerusalem, a city of undistinguished architecture—mostly drab, honey-colored stone—perched on a collection of dry hills. Unlike verdant Damascus, its vegetation was as homely as its buildings, mostly dusty olive trees and scrub bushes.

But if trees and gardens did not bloom there, temples did, for it was home to many faiths and a god was poor indeed if he had not at least one place of worship. Here was one dedicated to Jove, another to Astarte, there another for Diana, two for Mithras, over there one for Horus, and of course everywhere were statues and monuments to Caesar. Grandest of all was the temple built by Herod for the Jews themselves, where the two briefly stopped so Ismail could sacrifice a goat kid for his mother, as he had promised her spirit.

Afterwards, they made their way to a neighborhood near Damascus Gate, where Ismail had relatives who could provide them room and board. "Now that we are here, Master, how shall we find the child?" he inquired. "It seems to me that every third woman is a mother with children and every third child is a squalling babe. Did your scrolls tell you the family of the messiah?"

"They did not. But we won't find him here. The signs point elsewhere. We're here to consult Jewish seers. Your people have prophecies of their own and it was the hope of myself and the others that one of these would give the place of birth. I don't know if my fellow Magi are still here, but if not, perhaps they left word for me."

Jerusalem was crowded because a census commanded by Herod required every male citizen to return to the place of his birth and report to local authorities. The house of Ismail's cousin was packed with both distant relatives and paying guests, but somehow space was found for them and a corral for the camels.

The evening meal was a noisy, cramped affair, a dozen men sitting together in a room meant for half that number. The women, who ate in another room, brought in dishes that were plain but nourishing. Conversation was lively but there was a lull near the end of the meal, when they were full or overfull, and Artaban took the opportunity to ask about his friends. "Three priests of Zoroaster like myself. They would have arrived in a small caravan about two weeks ago. Does anyone have knowledge of them?"

"I heard about them," said a man across the table. "They've left, I think. There's a small market near here, ask about them there. Someone will either know or else know some other one who does."

The next day Artaban and Ismail circulated among the market stalls inquiring about the Magi but were met only with shrugs. By afternoon they had found one person who'd seen their arrival in the city and another who had seen them depart but that was all.

"I don't understand," said Artaban. "Three such as they couldn't have passed unnoticed, particularly if they were asking about prophecies of the messiah."

"Something's amiss," said Ismail. "I think at least some people have knowledge, but they're reluctant to tell what they know."

"But why?"

"No one wants to get in trouble with the Romans or Herod. Even talk of a messiah could be dangerous."

"You mean they might take us as spies seeking out sedition?"

"No, but they might be afraid to talk openly. Herod has little birds on every branch."

"Well, we must keep at it until we find someone."

"Master," said Ismail. "I think someone has found *us*." He pointed and Artaban saw the crowd parting for a squad of Roman soldiers headed their way. They had shields and spears and were led by a stout sergeant with a dour expression. Beside him walked a skinny fox-faced man who pointed at the two, then detached himself from the soldiers and vanished in the crowd.

The squad came to a halt before them. "You the two seeking the three Magi?" said the sergeant. It wasn't really a question.

"Who, us?" said Ismail. "We aren't—"

"Balthazar, Melchior and Caspar," said Artaban. "Priests of Zoroaster like myself. Do you know where they are?"

The sergeant motioned to his men. Soldiers stepped beside and behind them. "Come with me."

"What for? Are we under arrest?"

"Not unless you refuse to come."

"Where are you taking us?"

"The Palace."

"Why are we going there?"

"Great Jupiter, I don't know," the sergeant said wearily. "The captain told me Yusef the Weasel told him there were two men in the market by Damascus Gate asking about the Magi. He said to take four of the boys and Yusef would point them out. He said to bring 'em back. He didn't say why. He never does. Now you know as much as I do. I'd just as soon you come along peaceably but we can do it the other way if you like."

There was no point in resistance, so they went with the soldiers. A half-hour walk brought them to Herod's palace, an immense structure of gleaming white marble, the blocks so smoothly joined that it looked as though it was built of a single great stone. In that dry drab city it stood out not only for its splendor but its green surroundings. Canals carried well water to nourish its lush gardens and shady palm groves.

The soldiers took them around to a small door at the side. "Dungeon for sure," muttered Ismail.

"Why? They have no reason."

"Maybe not, but in my profession you expect the worst when you're in the hands of soldiers."

Inside, however, they were greeted with surprising courtesy by a Roman officer who dismissed the sergeant and his squad. He led them through winding hallways and up several flights of stairs, past pillars and porticos with busts of Jewish heroes and patriarchs.

"Well, Master," said Ismail. We're going up, not down, so at least we're not dungeon-bound."

"Dungeon?" said the officer. "No worry of that, fellow. The king wants to talk to your master."

He took them to a large room with couches and wall hangings where perhaps two dozen people chatted and laughed. At the far end was a throne on a dais, but it was empty. The officer beckoned a servant. "Tell the king that the priest of Zoroaster is here." He left and another servant offered them Cypriot wine while they waited.

In a little while, a noble in a dark purple robe with a patrician countenance appeared. "You are the Mage?" he asked in Hebrew, the language of the court.

"I am," Artaban replied. His Hebrew was rusty, less chance to practice it than Aramaic, but he could manage.

The noble told Artaban to come with him, an invitation that obviously didn't extend to his servant. Ismail, already in his second cup of Cypriot wine, happily stayed behind. Though he'd temporarily renounced his profession, he preferred by habit not to draw attention, being most content when he was least visible.

THEY crossed the large room and entered a smaller one even more richly furnished where the king held private councils. An old man, bald and immensely fat, sat on a cushioned chair, waited upon by a youth in a toga.

The noble sank to one knee and Artaban did likewise. "Majesty, this is the one you sent for."

"Rise," said Herod. "You may go, Tobit." The king gazed at Artaban with eyes encased in wrinkled flesh that glittered with shrewd intelligence. "You are a priest of Zoroaster?"

"I am, Majesty. My name is Artaban."

"The other Magi are known to you?"

"They are friends of mine. We were to travel together but I was delayed. Do you know where they are?"

"I know where they were headed."

"Where is—"

"Patience. I will tell you but in my own time. You and they are following the star."

"Yes."

"Seeking one destined to be king."

"The prophecies don't say 'king,' Majesty," Artaban said carefully. "They speak of a ruler but it's not clear if he would rule by law or otherwise."

"How else does a ruler rule?"

"He might be a ruler of the kingdom of the spirit, one who leads people to truth and righteousness."

"Your friends said something like that. That may be so but it's also the sort of thing one says to a sitting monarch. I think you and they worry I might intend ill to such a child – assuming there *is* such a child."

"Majesty, as King of Judea, I assume you have the best intentions toward all your people."

Herod's thin lips parted and emitted a wheezy cackle. "Oh, very clever! Your friends came up with nothing so good." He chuckled a moment longer and then the smile was gone. "Let me explain my interest in this babe, if he exists. We Jews have long expected a messiah who would lead us to a rebirth of our greatness. Whether he shall be a king, a general or as you say, a ruler of the spirit remains to be seen. Any king, though, would see him as a rival to the throne."

The old man gestured for his servant to hand him a goblet. His hand trembled and he drank slurpily. When he was done, the boy dabbed white drops from his mouth and whiskers.

"Goat's milk," Herod explained. "My doctors forbid me wine. My advice, Mage, is not to live after your time. As I was saying, any king would see this messiah as a threat – any *but* one in the last years of his life, whose nincompoop sons are bound to battle each other for the throne until Caesar steps in and settles matters to Caesar's liking. The Romans put me on this throne but you'd be surprised to hear I have no great love for them. If Judea is to be ever free of Rome's yoke, it will only come if she is led by a great ruler. Supposing this boy exists, he presents a better promise for this country than any of my own progeny."

Herod turned to the serving boy. "Give him the map."

The boy handed Artaban a scroll. He unrolled it to see a map of Judea.

"Our prophecies say the child will be born in a town, more a village really, about two days ride from here. The name of the place is Bethlehem. Do you see it?"

"Highness, the map is in a script I can't read."

"Point it out to him," Herod told the youth, who placed a finger on the map. "Do you wish a guide to lead you there?"

"My servant knows Judea well. He'll find it."

"As you wish. Bethlehem is a place of no distinction, but it's connected to the House of David. If the child's parents are from there, they're not likely to be people of wealth or standing. No child should be separated from his mother or father, but I wouldn't like to see him raised in rustic squalor. He should have education, not just in books but in how to conduct himself among the mighty. He must be prepared for his day of destiny."

Artaban handed the map back to the boy. "So your interest in this child is in seeing him properly raised."

"Not just raised properly but raised to rule," said Herod. "By the time he's old enough to make a claim to this throne—should he make it—I'll be long in my grave. But if he's to survive to that age, he must also be brought up far from here, in secrecy if possible. My children are as ruthless as any who aspire to a throne. And Rome is not likely to look kindly on one who might take Judea out of its orbit."

Herod began to cough. The boy gave him a cloth and he spat into it. "I said this same thing to your friends and told them to come back and tell me if they found the child. That was nearly two weeks ago but I haven't seen them since."

"Perhaps they didn't find him."

"Perhaps, but they must come through Jerusalem again if they're returning home, that is if they take the most direct route. I hope, Artaban, that *you* will return and tell me what you found, whether there is such a babe or not. And if you do find him, tell his parents that they need not fear Herod. Promise me you will do this."

"I promise, Majesty. Much glory will come to your name as the child's protector."

Herod smiled bitterly. "My life is so full of glory that I hardly need more." A drop fell from his nose. His servant handed him another a cloth and he loudly blew. "I am not much loved by my people. They think me Rome's tool. That I am, but I am not Rome's *fool*. Judea would been much worse off had I not been here to hold back Caesar's hand when he wished to squeeze us particularly tight. The people don't know that. They only know what happens, not what hasn't happened."

He was about to say more but was overcome by a new fit of coughing. He spat into the cloth he clutched in one hand and waved with the other for Artaban to depart. The Mage knelt and left.

# Chapter Ten

## Bethlehem

BACK in the throne room Artaban rejoined Ismail, who was all curiosity. "What did he—"

"Not here," Artaban answered. A servant led them out of the palace. When they were outside, Artaban asked Ismail if he knew the way to Bethlehem.

"I do. So the star leads to Bethlehem? Not a likely place to find one born to rule."

"Herod said as much. He also said he wanted to protect the child."

"From who? Herod?"

"He made a case that he'd rather be followed by a great leader than one of his 'nincompoop' sons. I'm not sure what to make of him."

"I can tell you what the people of Judea make of him. A cruel and corrupt despot."

"Doubtless, but an old one and he knows it. Even a bad king might love his country."

They took leave of Ismail's cousin early the next morning. The trip was uneventful, though twice they spotted a distant cloud of dust behind them. "Horses, I think," said Ismail the second time. "Camels don't kick up so much dust. Horses and a lot of them.

Either Romans or bandits is my guess. Do you want to leave the road?"

"If it's horses," replied Artaban, "why haven't they caught up with us by now?"

"A good question. They must be going slow, maybe on purpose. You suppose they're bound for Bethlehem too?"

"This road leads to other places than Bethlehem, doesn't it?"

"Many."

"Then it may just be coincidence. If Herod was after the child, surely he would have sent soldiers to follow Balthazar and the others."

"Maybe he doubted they'd found such a child. Might be now he's having second thoughts."

"Maybe. Whoever is behind us, whether following or not, there's nothing we can do about it. Let's go on."

The afternoon of the second day they came on shepherd boys driving sheep. "How far to Bethlehem?" Artaban asked.

"An hour more and you'll be there," said the oldest boy. "Are you from afar like the others?"

"What others?"

"Three on camels, like you. They came to see the baby."

"We saw the baby too," said another. "But the baby's very ordinary. Just another baby, nothing to travel a long way for."

"He may be just a baby," replied Artaban, "but if he is the child I seek, someday he will do great things."

"Maybe. Now the singing, *that* was something to travel for."

"What singing?"

"Singing all over. The same night the baby was born."

"Who was singing?"

"No one. No one we could see," said the third boy.

"But the sky was filled with song," said the first. "What wonderful song! Loud as thunder but not at all scary."

Artaban and Ismail looked at each other. "Is that in your scrolls?" said Ismail.

"No," Artaban replied, "but the scrolls speak of 'wonders.' Singing from on high, that is a wonder indeed."

"Are more coming like you?" asked a boy.

"No, I am the last."

"Well, *someone* is coming," said the boy, pointing.

They looked. The dust cloud had reappeared, this time closer.

"I don't like this," Artaban told Ismail. "Maybe it's soldiers bound for Bethlehem after all." He gave each of the boys a penny, which to them was a wonder all its own, and they hastened on.

They found Bethlehem a pleasant, quiet village. There was no one on the streets though. "My stomach tells me it's dinnertime," said Ismail. "They're all inside, either eating or getting ready to. Let's try a door."

They dismounted and went to a stone cottage. A woman's soft singing came from within. At Artaban's knock a pretty young woman came to the door.

"We're looking for a baby just born in this village," said Artaban.

"What? More of you?" answered the woman gaily. "So many fine visitors just to see a baby! Are there no babies where you come from?"

"None like this."

"That's what the others said. They said the singing was for him. Come in if you like. My husband's still in the field but you look safe enough. You must be quiet though. My own baby just went to sleep."

They stepped inside. "If it's a baby you've come to see," she said, "you may look at mine all you want. He's the sweetest, prettiest one in the whole town, and we have many. But if you're after the one the three others came to see, you're too late. They've gone on."

"My friends?"

"Them too, but I meant the family."

"Gone? Don't they live here?"

"No, they were travelers. There was no room for the man and his young wife but someone found them a stable. They were glad to get it but your friends were very offended to find the child keeping company with a cow! Have you brought fine presents like they did?"

But Artaban didn't hear the question. His shoulders sank and gloom settled on his face. "They've gone? Do you know where?"

"No, although some here heard them and the three talk of Egypt. So far away! But listen to me go on. Are the two of you hungry? I have food enough and let it never be said Rebecca, Isaac's wife, was poor in hospitality."

Artaban was too downcast to be hungry but a glance at Ismail told him his servant was famished. He accepted with an offer to pay but Rebecca wouldn't hear of it.

As she prepared plates, he gazed down at the slumbering boy, who had a red fuzz on his scalp. *Perhaps I'll have one like him in a year*, he thought. *Balthazar and the others gave their gifts to the promised one, but I'm too late. They must have warned the family about Herod. A man burdened with a wife and newborn won't travel too fast. They can't be far ahead. If I follow, I can overtake them before they've out of Judea.*

"The family," he said. "What are their names?"

"The man is called Joseph. His wife is Mary."

"And the baby? Have they named it yet?"

"Yes but it escapes me right now. Maybe it will come."

"Do you know what town they're from?"

"I don't recall. Won't you sit down? Supper's on the table."

The meal was simple but well-made and nourishing. "You have a very pretty child," Artaban remarked. "What do you call him?"

"Isaac. In my husband's family, the firstborn male has been named Isaac for generations. You have children?"

"Alas, no, but when I return home I hope to soon have a boy like your own. And a daughter. Many children."

"Where is your home?"

"Ecbatana. In Persia."

"You *have* traveled far! I've been to Jerusalem, no farther. What a mighty city!"

Ismail snorted but fell silent at a glance from Artaban. As the three ate, they chatted of the small things of daily life, such conversation as Artaban might someday have with Rasha, he thought wistfully.

When they had finished, Rebecca cleared the dishes. While she was away from the table, Ismail said quietly, "At least you needn't fear Romans will seize the child."

"No, but there's been more than enough time for whoever was behind us to reach the village. Perhaps it wasn't Herod's soldiers after all."

At that moment they heard a distant scream. Artaban stepped outside and saw Roman legionnaires. They were going from house to house, breaking down doors. Cries and wails rose from within the houses they entered. Down the street, a woman dashed from a doorway clutching an infant. Two soldiers caught up with her and tore the babe from her arms. Artaban gasped as he watched one of them thrust his blade into the tiny body. They strode away, leaving the distraught mother embracing her bloody child.

He quickly stepped inside and shut the door. "What's the matter? What's happening?" Rebecca asked fearfully.

"Romans. They're killing the children."

"Killing children! In God's name, why?"

"Not in God's name, Herod's I'm sure." He glanced about the house. It was a typical one-roomed village dwelling. There was nowhere to hide.

"They won't kill *my* child," Rebecca said, snatching up her son from his crib. "They'll have to kill me first."

"They will do that too if they need to. Wrap him up and crouch in the corner. Make yourself as small as possible. And keep him quiet. You must keep him quiet!" He turned to Ismail. "Stand in front of her. Shield her with your robe if you can."

"As you say, Master, but you know it will do no good," said Ismail, stepping in front of the cowering mother with her child.

Artaban looked at the door. It was a narrow, flimsy thing. The Romans would knock it down in half a minute. He flung it open and stood in the doorway, filling the frame. A brawny, grim-faced officer and several soldiers were already heading for the house.


THE name of the officer was Marcus Caius and over the years he'd done his share of killing, though never before children. It made him sick to his stomach, but the first lesson he learned when he enlisted was to follow orders. "Follow 'em exactly," said the tough old sergeant who gotten the skinny fifteen-year-old through his first year in the Legion. "Exactly, nothing more, nothing less."

Now he was in his twenty-second year, rising through the ranks to captain. He had a wife and three children in Rome, though he'd seen little of them for the last few years. The price of making captain was service abroad.

He little cared for the military but a man had to make a living and soldiering was all he knew. His wife's brother had apprenticed to a blacksmith and was now one himself with a small shop of his own. The last time Marcus Cais was home the two of them had talked of building a stable. A man with a stable could make real money. Neither had the capital though so the talk came to nothing.

Marcus Caius was surprised to see someone who was clearly neither Jewish nor a villager blocking his way, but he was undeterred. Orders were to look in every house. "Step aside," he told the stranger. "Step aside or die." He spoke Aramaic, though only passingly, enough to communicate with the people he encountered.

The stranger didn't flinch. "You look to be a man of intelligence," he said in Latin as smooth as any citizen of Rome, his voice calm and low. "Walk on and this is yours." He held out his right palm. What was in it sparkled blue in the sunlight.

Marcus Caius stared at the stone, then at the stranger, who stared back, then at the stone again. It was either a diamond or a sapphire, as big as any he'd seen adorning the women in Herod's palace. But he saw more than a jewel. He saw a turning point in his life, all for the price of a Jewish brat.

Marcus Caius' sergeant and three men stood behind him. "I'll do this place," he told the sergeant. "Take the men to the next one."

The sergeant had been long enough in the army to know when a bribe was about to pass hands, and because he'd been long in the army he also knew when it was best to be blind. He turned to the others. "Captain says do the next house," he told them, as he and the squad moved on.

Marcus Caius turned back to the stranger. "I have to come inside." He saw doubt in the stranger's eyes. "In case anyone's watching. Let me in."

The man moved from the doorway. Marcus Caius stepped inside. His eyes swept the room. Nothing to see but a few sticks of furniture and another man, the stranger's servant no doubt, standing in a corner. Someone was behind him. He had no desire to find out who. He sheathed his sword and held out his hand. The stranger put the stone in it.

Marcus Caius looked closely at the stone. He was no jeweler but it looked like the real thing. He turned and without another word walked out the door. He heard it shut behind him. Another squad of soldiers was approaching, swords drawn. "No brats in there," he told them. "Let's do the houses down the street and get out of this town before we all start puking."

He strode off and the soldiers followed. He was already composing the letter telling his wife he was quitting the army and coming home. He briefly wondered why a man would pay a prince's ransom for the life of a child not his own but he didn't ponder overlong. In the wink of an eye his life had changed and he had other things to think about.

THE killing went on for half an hour more. At length they heard the clatter of hooves, loud at first, then growing faint. Artaban stepped outside to see the soldiers were now no more than dust on the road.

Ismail joined him. "Where are they going? Jerusalem's the other way."

"Likely to the next village for more slaughter. Herod's casting his net far."

They saw several farmers, armed with scythes and hoes and other tools, running across the fields toward the village. More could be seen in the distance. A muscular red-haired young man was in the lead, his face full of anger. In few minutes he was barreling down the street toward them, threshing blade raised.

"Who are you?" he shouted. "By heaven, if you've hurt my family, you'll—"

"They *protected* us, Isaac," said Rebecca, appearing at the doorway clasping her son. She put her hand on Artaban. "Had it not been for this man…" She shuddered.

Isaac put his arms around his wife and child, embracing them and ushering them back inside. "What happened?" he said. "What were the Romans doing here?"

"Killing infants," said Artaban.

"*What?* That's madness. Whatever for?"

"Herod thinks it a precaution. The child that was born in the manger, the king is afraid he'll grow up to gain the throne."

"In that case," said Isaac darkly, "he can't grow up fast enough."

"The Romans have taken their butchery to other villages. When they're done, they'll come through Bethlehem again on their way back to Jerusalem. I doubt they'll stop, but just one squall from your son at the wrong time could be dangerous. If I were you, in the morning I'd take your family with you to the fields, at least for the next several days."

"I'll do that," said Isaac, arm around Rebecca. "Will the two of you stay tonight? We haven't much but what we have—"

"Thank you but no. I'm in search of this child myself. If we're to catch up with the family, we must be on our way."

Artaban and Ismail made hasty farewells and mounted their camels. The Bethlehem they left was much changed from the peaceful village they'd entered. On either side of them, lamentation and keening rose from the homes of tillers and tradesmen and cobblers and carpenters, simple ordinary people whose lives had been upended by the fears and schemes of the mighty.

"That was a fine thing you did, Master," said Ismail from his camel.

"A costly thing. Now I have only the pearl for the child."

A weeping man emerged from one of the houses holding a lifeless toddler with long flaxen hair. He kissed it over and over, its blood smearing his beard and shirt.

"That one's a girl," said Ismail. "No newborn either. Why would they kill her?"

"I doubt the Romans have more stomach for killing children than any other man. Likely they steel themselves, don't look close, just get it done fast as possible."

"A bad business," said Ismail from his camel. "Could be we're riding into danger ourselves."

"We might be," said Artaban. He turned in his saddle. "You've taken me to where the babe was born, just as you promised. You can go your own way now." He smiled. "If your mother calls on you, tell her to visit me and I'll say you've served me well."

"Master, what I said was 'till we found the babe.' Once we have, I'll be on my way."

"That could be months."

"I'm in for it as long as you are."

"That will be no more than half a year at most, even if we haven't found him. My betrothed said she would wait that long and no longer. I'll give up a jewel for this child but not the woman I love."

"Sounds like a woman of spirit."

"A jewel all her own, Ismail. As for him we seek, I hope to have a look at him before I turn home. If he can unsettle a king when he's a few days old, what may he do as a man?"

"A mighty warrior, you mean?"

"Mighty but maybe not a warrior. He might be a teacher or a seer. The prophecies of your people speak of a messiah."

"My people and prophets have talked of a messiah since Methuselah was a tot – a leader who will smite Rome or Egypt or Babylon or whoever has his foot on our heads. Every now and then someone shows up and says, *'That's me.'* We Jews are a gullible lot so we take him at his word until he gets his own head chopped off, usually with a lot of us too."

"A messiah doesn't have to be a general or lead an army. He could be a man of peace."

"Not that I would differ with a learned man like yourself, Master, but it's my observation that in this world, men of peace get cut in pieces when they get in the way of kings and emperors. Little children too. A shame we never found out the babe's name."

"You're right, Ismail! We didn't. The killings drove it from my mind."

"We could still ask."

"No, we should leave these people to their sorrow – and their anger. The longer we stay, the more likely some will realize the Romans arrived less than an hour after we did. They may turn their anger on us."

"You're right there. Man with a dead child wants somebody to pay, and we're handier than Herod."

"We're sure to discover his name eventually. They can't be more than a few days ahead of us."

So the two rode away from Bethlehem to the sound of mourning and laments. A cold rain began to fall, as if the heavens, so lately in miraculous song, had joined in the little town's weeping.

# Chapter Eleven

## Egypt

DESPITE Artaban's optimism, they failed to catch up with the fleeing family, which seemed to have vanished. He conjectured they'd had sold one of their gifts for passage by caravan or even bought a horse and cart, which would convey them faster than a man with a woman on a donkey.

At length he and Ismail passed from Judea into Egypt, scanning the road and asking at inns for a family of three: a man named Joseph, a woman named Mary and a newborn whose name they didn't know.

Artaban's Egyptian was rusty but it came back with each day. They stopped at Heliopolis, a green and ancient town shaded by spreading sycamores, but if the family of Joseph had spent time there, no one noticed. After a week, they went on until they came to great and sprawling Memphis. There they found more than one neighborhood of Jewish families and not a few with newborns, but none that was the one they sought. From time to time they came across neighbors or shopkeepers who remembered a man they thought named Joseph with a wife they thought named Mary with, yes, a male newborn whose name was John or Jacob or James or Jesse, something like that, but, well, they had moved on some time ago.

"At least we know they're in Egypt," said Artaban after one such exchange.

"If the man's name was Joseph and not Jonah," said Ismail. "If the woman's name was Mary and not Martha. If their child was a boy and not a girl. Babies look alike, you know."

After weeks in Memphis they gave up and journeyed on to Thebes, along the way pausing to marvel at the pyramids and their vigilant stone guardian, the Sphinx. "Half man and half lion," observed Artaban. "A fearsome creature but of two natures."

"Man or lion, which is the more fearsome?" replied Ismail. "Is he smiling, would you say?"

"He might be."

"A smile's friendly but somehow not on him."

"There's a story that goes with the sphinx. It guarded a bridge that a traveler had to cross—"

"The river's a long way from here, Master,"

"This was another sphinx."

"There's more than one? How do they breed?"

"They breed in the imagination of men, which begets more monsters than ever dwelt in river or wood. As I said, this one guarded a bridge and travelers had to answer his riddle or be devoured. No one had ever answered the riddle."

"What was it?"

"What walks on four legs in the morning, two at noon and three at dusk?"

"Lucky we came on this one and not the other or I'd be sphinx food for sure. Do you know the answer?"

"The answer is 'man.' In the morning of life, he crawls. At noon, he walks. And as night draws close, he leans on a cane."

"And is that the answer the traveler gave?"

"It is."

"And the sphinx let him pass?"

"The sphinx threw itself off the bridge."

"Shouldn't play such games if it takes losing so hard. So why do you think this sphinx is smiling?"

"Perhaps that's *his* riddle. Perhaps he smiles to see those like us who come to stare at him and wonder why he smiles."

"If Joseph and his family came this way, they might have stopped and stared at this very spot."

"So they might, and I suppose if we're to find them, we should be on our way."

But they failed to find the family in Thebes as well. After a time they continued south, keeping to the banks of the Nile, seeking and asking in river towns and fishing villages, sometimes finding traces of such a family, but like footprints on a sandy shore, they always vanished before they could be followed.

Weeks passed and the land around the river, except for narrow strips of green shoreline, grew browner and drier until it turned into desert. Ismail surveyed the desiccated scene and shook his head. "If they came this way, I think they went no further south."

"I think you're right. We should turn back."

"And then where?"

"Alexandria. It's bigger than Memphis or Thebes, the biggest port in this part of the world. If the family has left Egypt, they may well have gone by sea. And if they did, they went through Alexandria. We'll sell the camels and go back by boat. Mayhap they did too. We'll quiz river travelers."

After five months, Artaban's money belt had grown thinner so they finally settled on a dismal craft that took passengers when the freight trade was light. The vessel was a shallow-draft Egyptian ship called the *Lucky Lady*, or so its name was translated to them in the Nile dialect that the diverse peoples of the river used instead of their native tongue, whether Egyptian, Greek, Jewish, Persian, Roman, Assyrian or otherwise. The crew later informed Ismail that "Loose Lady" was a more accurate translation, and more accurate still was a particular gesture used by riverfront prostitutes to advertise their wares.

Lucky or Loose, their ship was not a fast lady, docking several times a day to load and unload. To her passengers, her progress seemed slower every day. Their accommodations were cramped and since the ship was old and leaky, all hands, including passengers, had to take turns manning the pumps just to keep her afloat. The diet was monotonous, every meal fried fish and rice. Winter was long past; the weather had turned warm; mosquitos were thick and everyone on board grew rank. The crew was a rude and rowdy lot that Artaban avoided, though Ismail took to them.

The confinement and boredom and bugs and stink took their toll on master and servant. Ismail increasingly spent his evenings in the company of the crew while Artaban, in the narrow room that passed for their cabin, could hear the sounds of drink and gambling. He said nothing until one morning after Ismail had stumbled in the night before, clearly the worse for wine.

"I take a glass now and then myself," he said as they ate their breakfast of fried fish and rice. "If a man chooses to drink overmuch, I say nothing so long as he can do his job."

"You've found no reason to complain of my service," Ismail said surlily.

"No, I haven't. Besides, your head the next morning is more punishment than I could mete out, but when I took you on, I told you no thieving and no gambling."

"I haven't thieved!" Ismail said hotly.

"I don't say you have, but you've gambled, haven't you?"

"Only a little, just to pass the time with the boys. It's something to do."

"It's folly. By your own account you've spent long years with the bones. You know how to read the odds and how to read men. You're bound to win more than they do."

"I let them win too."

"This isn't some inn where you can slip away in the night. We're here until Alexandria. Even the dullest of them will start to see the pattern, and like all men that lose at gambling they'll suspect you cheat."

"I don't cheat!"

"Of course you do. Every man that makes his living by gambling cheats when luck goes against him, as it surely must at times."

"All right, maybe I improve the odds sometimes but, like you said, I can read men. I know when they're watching me, waiting to catch me. I never take a dumb chance."

"Ismail, for a man like yourself there is no kind of chance *but* dumb chance. When we go counter to the laws of the One, we step away from the guidance of the kindly sun and into the shadow of the Other, who waits to snare the unwary by—"

"Save your sermons for the temple and make your point."

"Very well. Here's my point. I said no gambling and no thieving and you said, 'yea, Master.' I know that's your profession, so called. How you made your living before my service—or how you make it *after* my service—is not my affair. But I won't have you doing either while we're on this boat. Cheating is no more than thieving by another name. If you can't abide by that, I'll pay you such wages as I owe and you can leave the next time we dock."

Ismail was silent for a long minute. "All right," he said finally. "Those were your terms and I agreed to them. Let me have one last game with the lads tonight so I can lose big. That way they won't resent it when I stop spending my evenings with them."

"Agreed. Letting them win some of their money back is a wise course, but you can spend your evenings as you like, with them if you choose."

"I can't spend time with them and not drink and dice. That's all they know. It's a hard life. They sweat all day, lifting and hauling. Wine and the bones are the only thing to look forward to. Lately the only thing *I've* looked forward to. You have your magic glass, so you're happy to spend hours looking at the everlasting stars. You've let me look through it and they're pretty, I admit. But, Master, how a man can occupy himself that way night after night is beyond me. Alexandria can't come too soon."

"There are mysteries in the stars, Ismail. Sometimes there are even answers. But, yes, I yearn for land too."

So master and servant mended their friendship, at least for the time. The days and nights passed slowly but pass they did and in another week, they made the port of Alexandria, there to begin again their round of inquiries: *a man named Joseph, his wife named Mary, a small baby, maybe six months old...*

# Chapter Twelve

## Partings

NINE days they spent seeking Joseph's family when, at the end of another fruitless day, Artaban saw a familiar face in the seaport's milling throng. "Hamid!" he cried jubilantly. The other turned and on spotting Artaban, his face split with a grin. They plowed through the throng to embrace and pound each other on the back.

"What are you doing here, old friend?" asked a beaming Artaban.

"Buying silk and spice for the ladies of Ecbatana," said the short, plump merchant with a grin. "They make their men pay handsomely for pretty clothes and flavorful food. And you? I'd heard you'd gone off on a quest, something about that wandering star. Are you still at it?"

"For a while yet. I promised the daughter of Tigranes I would be home by the cusp of Aries, when day and night are equal, but that is long passed. She said she would wait for me six months and no longer. " He laughed. "A strong-willed girl and I dare not defy her! How is she, do you know?"

Hamid's face grew long. Vendors and buyers and slaves laden with goods flowed busily around them. "Let us step out of the crowd," he said. "There is some space to breathe over there."

"What is it?" Artaban said anxiously as they made their way to a spot away from the traffic. "Something's amiss, isn't it? Rasha's not wed, has she? Surely not! Is another man openly courting her? Well, she's a girl and young, but how could Tigranes allow that? He'd not go back on his word. Tell me, what is it?"

Hamid drew a deep breath. "Rasha is gone, my dear friend."

"Gone where? Far?"

"Gone to where none return. Some months ago a fever swept through the city, not a full plague, but bad. It was gone in a few weeks but it took many with it. Rasha was one."

"Dead?" said Artaban. "She is dead?" His legs grew weak and he might have collapsed had not Ismail caught him and helped him to a nearby crate. "Surely not? Not my Rasha. She's too strong, too lively! It must have been one of Tigranes' other daughters, poor thing. I am sorry to hear it but it could not have been Rasha."

"I heard it from Tigranes himself, my friend. It was quick. He said one morning she could not get out of bed and by nightfall she was dead. The city had corpse carts collecting bodies for quick burials but the family hid her death and quietly put her to rest themselves." He gripped Artaban by the shoulder. "I am very sorry."

Artaban's face was pale and stricken. "I cannot believe it," he said. "Rasha can't be dead. She had so much life! So much…" His voice trailed away.

Hamid embraced Artaban but the other didn't respond. His gaze was blank and his arms hung limp.

114

After a few moments, the merchant excused himself to return to his work. He looked at Ismail. "You are his friend?"

"His servant. My name is Ismail."

"I'll be here for another few days. I will call on him. Where are you staying?"

"At the Inn of the Dolphin. It's just off Wide Street near the temple of Isis."

Hamid nodded and left. Ismail guided his master, who seemed like one in a dream, to the inn.

If Artaban slept that night, Ismail didn't know it. He looked into his master's room several times. Artaban had not moved from the chair where he sat, staring at nothing, his food untouched.

Yet when Ismail rose the next morning, the room was empty. He went downstairs, where the innkeeper told him that his master had left just after daylight, saying only that he would be back in a few hours.

Ismail ate breakfast and spent the morning in idle chat with the servants of other guests until Artaban strode through the inn door just before noon. Ismail rose. "Where have you been, Master?"

"Searching for Joseph's family, of course." He sat at a table and ordered a midday meal for both of them. Ismail was glad to note that although Artaban didn't eat heartily, he did at least eat. Artaban pushed his plate away early but waited patiently until Ismail was done.

"Let's be off," he said, rising. "We have yet to make inquiries on the south side of the city and that will take us the better part of another week."

Ismail rose but the perplexity in his face was evident. "What is it?" asked Artaban briskly.

"Nothing, except... Well, I thought you might want to visit the Temple of Fire. There's one here, you know."

"I did that this morning," said Artaban. "I lit a flame for Rasha and said a prayer. More I cannot do."

"I see."

"You seem puzzled."

"I suppose I am, Master, though it's none of my business."

"Go on."

"Yesterday you were a man adrift. You couldn't eat, couldn't sleep, had no words for anyone."

"I had just learned my betrothed was dead."

"Exactly. You behaved as any man would. Yet today..."

"Today I seem to have forgotten about her."

"No, of course not. I know you haven't. Yet, are you... ready to... continue?"

"Today I am as devastated as I was yesterday. I eat because I must, though I have no appetite. Tonight I am sure I will sleep, at least a little. If it would bring Rasha back, I would not eat or sleep ever again. But I can't. Meanwhile, the child and his family slip farther from us with each day. I must find him. I *shall* find him. That I can do, though my heart is, as you say, adrift... on a sea of sorrow."

Ismail said nothing to this and followed silently as Artaban left the inn.

THEY continued their search. The days passed. True to his word, Hamid came by and he and Artaban shared a meal at a tavern, talking of mutual friends and events in Ecbatana since the Mage had left. Or rather Hamid talked; Artaban listened attentively but with only an occasional question or comment. They did not speak of Rasha again, except once when Artaban handed him a letter of consolation for Tigranes.

The next morning at breakfast Artaban said, "I do not think they are here, though we've come across several who remember them."

"One wasn't sure of the child's age, another of the child's sex."

"And one said the child was a boy, about six months old. He is about that age by now."

"Yes but she saw them three months ago."

"Some children grow fast. In any case, they've moved on. I think they have left Asia."

"For where?"

"Greece. There are many Jews there. Maybe Joseph or Mary had relatives. That's where we'll go. You continue to search the neighborhood we started yesterday. I'll find us a ship bound for Athens. We'll start there."

Ismail put down his spoon and took a breath. "When you do, book only passage for one."

"I'm sorry to hear you say that," Artaban replied quietly. "I will miss you. You've served me well."

"I've been fortunate. You're a good man and a good master. If I may, let me speak to you now as a friend."

"Speak."

"Give this up. Go back to Ecbatana and take up your life. In time, the pain of losing Rasha will pass. You're yet young. You said Rasha had sisters. They'll be of an age to marry before…"

Artaban shook his head. "I could never—"

"You feel that way now. Of course you do, but that may change. In any case, take up your studies again. You're a priest of Zoroaster. Go back to spreading his teachings. Conduct services at the Temple of Fire. Do what you will, but whatever you do, don't waste more time in this futile quest."

"It is not futile."

"If Joseph's family could be found, we would have found them by now, at the least come across someone who knew them."

"We *have*."

"We've spoken with people who remember families *like* Joseph's. How many such families are there? Too many to count! Every family, however big, starts off with a mother, a father and a child. Never yet have we encountered someone who has said, 'Yes, *them*. I remember them well. Their son was born in Bethlehem.' Myself, I think the Romans caught up with them and slew the child, not because they knew who he was but because he was a newborn. Joseph may have tried to stop them. Likely he did, just like any father would. They may have slain him too. Whatever happened, chances are this family of three is now only two, maybe one or none."

"No," said Artaban with conviction. "The child escaped. Somehow. I'm sure of it. He was fated, destined. The prophecies—"

The prophecies spoke of a child born under a star. How many towns fell under that star? How many babies?"

"The Jewish prophecies spoke of Bethlehem."

"There are prophecies and there are prophecies. Who's to know which are right? Who's to say those prophecies are not for one yet to be born?"

"They spoke of wonders. When this boy was born there was singing from above."

"Was there? You and I never heard it. All we know is what the shepherd boys told us. Maybe Balthazar and the others spoke to them of wonders, and later the boys took the wind for song. They *were* boys and boys have wonderful imaginations. Maybe they told us of wonders because we expected to hear of wonders. Maybe they told us and later laughed at us for fools."

"There *was* a family. The mother gave birth in a manger."

"I don't doubt there was a family, nor that they had reason to flee. That doesn't mean their son was 'born to rule,' only that a superstitious old man named Herod had been visited by Persian priests who fed his superstitions."

"The boy *was* born. He *is* the one of the prophecies," said Artaban with a firm voice. "And I *will* find him, if it takes the rest of my life."

"And so it will if he doesn't exist, but even if he does, *why?* To give him a pearl of rare value? Forgive me, but this is a great deal of trouble for a late birthday present. If the child is who you think, he will reveal himself in time. You will hear of him. Go then and present him this gift when he is older and can appreciate its value."

"Wise advise, Ismail," said Artaban in a calm voice. "for any other man, but I cannot give up. Just as he is fated, so am I. He was destined to be born under the star. I was destined to follow it and find him. I cannot rest until I do."

"The wandering star has wandered on," said Ismail, his own voice rising. "It has not shone for months. What did it mean? Maybe it meant nothing!"

Artaban said naught to this and his silent resistance seemed to goad Ismail more than any argument. "You are a man of faith. The teachings of Zoroaster guide your steps. I admit that I am not. There are too many gods to believe in them all and how is a man to know which are real, if any? What do I know of fate? My own destiny is to be hungry at noon and to want a woman at night. If I have another, it hasn't shown itself."

He locked eyes with Artaban and spoke with such passion that the people in the inn turned to stare. Servants didn't speak to masters this way, not those that wanted to stay employed. For that matter, friends rarely spoke to friends this way. There was a heat to Ismail's words that was like the kind of dispute brothers might have, something about more than the matter of the moment, something that spoke of deep affection or resentment. "If a man chooses to believe in fate, fine, so long as his fate is kind to him. But when your fate fails to serve you, it's time to find a new one."

Artaban met Ismail's gaze. He didn't look away but neither did he respond. His resolve seemed rooted in something beyond explanation, beyond appeal.

Ismail grew red in the face. "This destiny of yours is a delusion. It has a kind of grandeur but it's folly just the same. At first I thought a man of learning like you must know things I don't, understand things I can't. Then as time went by I saw that you groped in the dark as much as any man. I can't tell you how it pains me to see someone I admire and respect and... *like* throw his time away on such lunacy."

Ismail stood. Artaban did not rise, nor did he raise his eyes to meet the other's. Ismail set a coin on the table. "Here is money for my meal. I am my own man again and I pay for what I eat. Farewell, Artaban the Mage. You saved my life and for that I am forever grateful, but I will not cast my lot with a man who throws away his life on a fool's quest. Be the fool of fate if you will, but I will not be *your* fool!"

He strode to the door and left. Artaban stared straight ahead. After a moment the other diners looked away, puzzled or embarrassed. After a while the Mage put down money for his meal and walked out.

# Chapter Thirteen

## Bones

THE DAYS passed, yet Artaban lingered in Alexandria. He revisited those with vague memories of the family and explored neighborhoods he and Ismail had overlooked. He spent time with various Greeks who advised him where those in flight from Herod's agents might take refuge. Once he went to the Temple of Fire and lit a flame, sitting quietly for hours.

The nights were mild and in the evenings he sometimes strolled the streets, sampling the city's jostling sounds and smells and sights. The taverns were always crowded with sailors singing and gambling and occasionally brawling. One night a door opened and a gang of men erupted into the street, grappling with someone in their midst. Artaban was barely able to dodge them as they tumbled out, yelling and cursing. "Hold him!" roared a short, muscular man with flaming red hair and a booming voice. "Don't let him get away!"

"We got him!" yelled back someone.

"Get him inside!" said the red-haired sailor.

"Not in here," declared a barrel-chested man who appeared in the doorway. "I run an alehouse, not a fighting pit. You got a quarrel, settle it elsewhere."

"Oh, we'll settle it all right," said the sailor. "No one cheats Red Khamet and gets away with it!"

"That's none of my affair," said the owner, who went back inside, slamming the door.

"Hold out his arm," ordered Red Khamet. "Not that one, you dolt! His *right* arm. Hold it straight." He drew a large, ugly blade from his belt. "Your cheating days are done, you scab of a thief!"

Artaban gazed with disgust and mounting alarm at the sight. The captive was about to lose his thumb or a pair of fingers, the usual street penalty for cheating gamblers. He loathed the brutal punishment, but violence was common in a city of such size and energy and in any case there was nothing he could do. A priest of Zoroaster held little sway with such men, even those that might profess to follow the One. They'd all been drinking and were inflamed with rage. He walked around the melee and continued on until a voice made him stop and turn.

"I didn't cheat!"

Artaban stared, stunned. The man in the center of the brawl, struggling against others who wrestled to keep him still, was Ismail.

"Those are honest bones," Ismail cried. "Your own!"

"Honest they may be," said Red Khamet, "but you're *not*. Hold him still, boys. I don't want to cut the wrong man." He raised his knife.

In that moment, time froze for Artaban and his mind was churned by a dozen thoughts, his heart by a dozen emotions. What should he do? What could he do? Why do anything? He had saved this scoundrel's life once, only to be repaid with the theft of his gems.

True, the man had repented and returned the stones but not before gambling away one of them forever. Yes, Ismail had been a dutiful servant, even an honest one, which must have been a struggle for one of his nature. The truth was he was a knave. He stole without remorse, cheated and lied without shame, even discomfort. He recognized no deity, nothing higher than his own appetites, which were common and base: gambling, drink, women. He had no conscience and feared only the wrath of his mother, or rather her spirit.

Artaban was not glad to see Ismail in this dilemma but he recognized its rude justice. It had only been a matter of time until the man's misdeeds caught up with him. It was a great sorrow but Artaban had no way to save him. Even if he had, he was under no obligation, not even that of friendship. Ismail had torn whatever affection the Mage felt for him with his final words, calling him a fool on a lunatic quest. The derision of one who had shared the months of searching still stung. Whatever was about to happen, Ismail had brought on himself. Artaban could go on without shame or regret. He should have gone on six months before, on the road to Borsippa.

So it was that Artaban was surprised to hear his own voice call out, "Stay your hand."

More surprised was he to see Red Khamet do just that. He held the blade high but turned his head to the speaker. He was not a man easily intimidated and he wasn't intimidated now but there was an authority in Artaban's voice that made him hesitate.

"Who are you?" he growled.

"I am Artaban the Mage."

"A wizard?" said Red Khamet a little worriedly.

"I don't dabble in sorcery. I'm a priest of Zoroaster. This man was once my servant. You say he cheated you?"

"I *know* he cheated me. I caught him at it."

"I never cheated!" cried Ismail.

"Shut up, you," snarled Red Khamet to Ismail. "Or I'll cut off more than your hand."

"You intend to cut off his entire hand?" said Artaban, shocked.

"That I do."

"That will kill him."

"Maybe. Maybe you can save his worthless life with your arts."

"How much did he cheat you?"

"None," said Red Khamet, holding up a sack of coins. "I got it all back. It's not the theft. It's the disrespect. I won't have anyone making a fool of me. Ask the boys."

"That's so," said one of his gang. "Nobody messes with Red."

"Nobody," agreed another.

"Are you done, Mage?" said Red Khamet. "I only talk to you out of respect, for I can see you're a man of learning. Go or stay, but don't delay me any longer."

Artaban had briefly considered paying Red Khamet whatever sum he claimed Ismail had cheated, but it was obvious such an offer was pointless. He quickly appraised Red Khamet. He wasn't a big man; he was shorter than most of his gang. He led by force of personality. He was proud to the point of arrogant, not one to back down or be bought, especially in front of his gang. Yet his pride offered a leverage. He was the kind of man who might respond to a challenge.

"Hold your hand a moment longer and there may be something in it for you," said Artaban.

Red Khamet snorted. "Such as?"

"You were throwing the bones?"

"We were."

"You're a man who likes to gamble."

"What of it? Are you going to sermonize me on the evils of gambling?"

"No. I'm going to propose a wager."

Red Khamet looked doubtful. "What sort of wager?"

"We'll throw the bones... for his hand."

Red Khamet stared at Artaban, dumbfounded. Then he laughed, a harsh barking noise without any mirth in it. His gang laughed as well, though there was more merriment in their voices. Artaban said nothing more but kept his eyes on Red Khamet. After a moment, the sailor stopped laughing, though a cold smile stayed on his lips. "Not interested."

"You haven't seen what I'll put up for stakes."

"Show me," Red Khamet sneered. The sneer faded when Artaban reached under his robe and a moment later held out a pearl. "You're joking!"

"No," said Artaban.

Red Khamet and his gang stared at the jewel. One of the men softly swore. "Biggest pearl I've ever seen."

"That it is," said Red Khamet. His face darkened. "Is it real?"

"It is."

"You swear? This is no jape?"

Artaban shook his head. "No jape. We'll play one game. Just the two of us. If I win, he keeps his hand."

"And if I do?"

"The pearl is yours, the hand too."

"You'd do this for a servant?"

"I would."

"Why? Did he save your life once?"

Artaban suppressed a bitter smile. "My reasons are my own. Do we have a bet?"

"Swear by your god this pearl is real."

"In the name of the One, who sets all in motion and ends all our days, this is a true pearl."

Red Khamet, who had held his blade over Ismail's wrist for their entire conversation, slid the knife back in his belt. He held out his own big, calloused hand to Artaban. "Shake on it, Mage."

Artaban clasped Red Khamet's hand in his own. The man's grip was bone-crushing but he hid his pain. "We have a bet," announced Red Khamet, looking around for the first time. They'd drawn a small crowd. "Problem. We can't play here in the street and Hama won't let us back in his tavern."

One of his gang pointed to an alley between the tavern and a butcher shop. "We can do it there, Red."

Red Khámet grunted an assent and they moved to the alley. Someone produced a pair of tar torches that provided enough light to play by. Two big sailors gripped Ismail by his arms and the gang formed a ring around Artaban and Red Khamet. The crowd followed, overflowing into the street. Artaban could hear spectators talking to one another and after a moment he realized bets were being placed.

"We need a stake holder," one of the men said.

"For what?" growled Red Khamet.

"Well," said the other hesitantly, "it's just common, you know, when strangers play."

"This man's a priest of the Sun God. That's good enough. And my stakes are right *here*," he said, touching Ismail's arm, held tightly by his guards. Ismail flinched.

Red Khamet turned to Artaban and grinned. "I don't suppose you brought your own bones, Mage."

"No."

"All right to play with mine?"

Artaban glanced at Ismail, who gave a small nod. "Yours will be all right."

Red Khamet held out two small white cubes. Artaban saw he was supposed to take the cubes and examine them, which he did, though he had no idea what he should look for. Each side of each cube had one or more black dots: two on one side, three on another and so on up to six. After a moment, he handed the cubes back to Red Khamet.

One of the gang used his knife to score a rude circle in the ground. Red Khamet sank to his knees just outside it and Artaban did the same. "When was the last time you played?" Red Khamet asked.

"I haven't."

"Haven't what?"

"Haven't played."

"Ever?" said Red Khamet in a tone of disbelief.

"Never."

Red Khamet and his men exchanged looks of amazement. "Not even as a boy, just for fun?"

"As a boy I spent my time in study." It occurred to him that to men like these, the idea of reading was foreign enough but spending a childhood reading verged on incredible. "Sometimes I rode my pony ," he added, then realized that to them this was no less strange.

They stared at Artaban as though he were a unicorn. "Well," said Red Khamet. "It's simple enough. It's all luck and, uh, feeling. Sometimes you get a feeling, hard to explain. But there's no skill as such to it. You've as much chance to win as me, even if you never played before. Here's how it goes. When we toss, the bones have to land inside the circle. One goes out and it don't count. What you do is toss the bones and the sides that show, you add 'em together to get your number. You might have two, might have twelve, might have anything in between. Some numbers are easier to make than others. There's only one way to make two or twelve but you can make seven three ways. You follow?"

"One and six, two and five, three and four," said Artaban.

"That's right. You're quick for a man of learning. Meaning no disrespect."

"None taken."

"So our first round is to decide the point. The 'point' is what we call the number to get. Suppose I toss and up comes six. Then you toss and up comes eight. That means the point is eight."

"Because eight is higher?"

"Right."

"Does that mean I win?"

"No, all the first round decides is the point we play for. We toss again and whoever makes the point first wins. Unless he throws seven."

"What happens if he does that?"

"He loses. Seven's the jinx."

"What happens if the point is seven?"

"Never is. When we throw to decide the point, if either us throws seven, we do it over."

"All right, what if it's your turn and you toss eight before I toss? Don't I get a chance to tie you?"

"No, not the way we usually play. We can do it that way though. Some like that better, makes it more interesting, you might say."

"It seems more fair."

"Course it works that way for me too. You come up eight but I ain't throwed yet, I get a chance."

"Of course. So what happens if we tie?"

"We toss again till one comes up eight and the other don't."

"And then?"

"That's it. Game's over. Like I said, it's simple. You ready to play?"

"One thing more. You said if a cube lands outside the circle, it doesn't count."

"Right."

"Does that mean we do the round over?"

"No, it just means you're stuck with one cube. Whatever shows is your number. Suppose the point's eight. You throw. One of your cubes comes up five. The other comes up three but it lands outside the circle. You've thrown eight but only the five counts, so you don't win."

"And if I throw five and two, but the two lands outside the circle?"

"Same thing. You've thrown seven. That's the jinx, but since only the five counts, you don't lose. You follow?"

"I follow. I'm ready to play."

"You want to roll first or you want me to?"

"I will."

Red Khamet handed the bones to Artaban. Someone produced a tin cup, which he also gave Artaban.

"What do I do with this?" Artaban asked.

There were snickers in the ring of spectators. "You put the bones in there," Red Khamet explained. "Shake 'em as much as you want, then toss 'em out."

Artaban dropped his cubes in the cup, shook it twice and tossed. One cube showed four and the other showed two.

"Six," said Red Khamet. "My turn now." He took the cup from Artaban and picked up the bones, which he lightly touched to his lips before dropping them in the cup.

"Why did you do that?" asked Artaban.

"Do what?" said Red Khamet.

"You kissed them."

"Oh," said Red Khamet with a look of embarrassment. "Do it so much I don't think about it. Gamblers are... well, we're superstitious, you might say. Got all sorts of things we do to woo Miss Luck to our side. I don't know if kissing the bones brings me luck, but what I do know is every now and then I forget to kiss 'em and when that happens, I lose. *Every* time."

"I see," said Artaban.

"Being a priest of the Sun God and all, you probably think that's pagan nonsense."

"Zoroaster taught that no man's beliefs are nonsense, not to him."

Red Khamet looked surprised and pleased at such open-mindedness. He tossed the bones, which came up five and six. "Eleven," he said. "Eleven's our point. Hard point to make. Only the one way to make it." He handed the cup to Artaban. "More likely one of us will make seven before then."

"And whoever makes seven loses the game?" said Artaban, gathering the bones.

"Right, so if you want to win, just make sure you don't make seven before I do."

"Sound advice," said Artaban. He dropped the two cubes in the cup and placed his hand over the top, whispering, *"O child born under the star, the pearl is rightfully yours. Forgive me for wagering it to save one unworthy, but he is near and you are far. May the One decide if my folly shall be rewarded or punished."* Then he tossed.

"Two and one," said Red Khamet. "Three. My turn." He took the cup. "Was that for luck, what you said just now?"

Artaban was about to explain that in his faith, it was a sacrilege to ask for luck or a blessing, that the One would decide what was right with wisdom superior to any mortal. Then he decided that was condescending, so he simply replied "In a way."

Red Khamet kissed the bones and tossed and made six. Since neither made eleven or jinxed with seven, they played again.

They played three more rounds without winning or jinxing and the crowd, which at first was noisy with comments and bets, had grown tensely quiet. He scanned the taut faces that looked down on him and Red Khamet, the torchlight flickering over their rough features. Artaban wondered how many were betting on him. Red Khamet would be the crowd favorite but maybe some of them liked the odds. They'd win bigger if he did.

He had avoided looking at Ismail during the game, which would have only distracted him, but now he allowed himself a quick glance. The man's brows were knotted, his eyes wide with fear, his forehead damp with sweat. A gang member on either side tightly held his arms. His right hand, the one he would lose if the bones went against him, was clenched into a fist.

A bead of sweat dropped onto Artaban's arm. He touched his hand to his forehead. It was as damp as Ismail's.

"Ten," growled Red Khamet, glaring at the cubes he'd just thrown. "That's twice I've made ten. Made twelve the time before. I can make the number in front of eleven and the one after it, but damnit, Miss Luck, what I want is eleven itself, if you please." He handed the cup to Artaban.

Artaban tossed. The bones came up three and four. Seven. Artaban stared at them blankly for a second, only thinking that again he'd failed to make eleven.

Then the import of seven hit him. *Seven.* Jinxed! He'd lost! Lost not only was his gift for the child but Ismail's right hand and likely his life. Grief and rage swelled up in Artaban in equal measure, grief at what had been lost and rage at the turn of events that had thrown his life upside-down. He looked at Ismail, whose eyes brimmed with tears. He heard cheers and groans in the crowd and a hearty chortle from Red Khamet.

"Hold it," said someone. "One's on the line!" A murmur ran through the crowd. Artaban looked down. One cube, showing three, had landed well inside the circle but the other, showing four, had landed on the line itself, neither fully in or out of the circle.

"On the line, it's still in play," said one of Red Khamet's gang. "Counts as seven. He's jinxed."

"Bull," responded someone in the crowd. "On the line is same as *out* of the line! He threw three. Roll again."

The spectators quickly divided into two camps, each loudly arguing the significance of a cube on the line.

Artaban looked at Red Khamet, who so far had said nothing. He stared intently at the cube, as if he could will it to move ever so slightly outside the circle. He raised his eyes and looked at Artaban, then surveyed the crowd. It was clear to Artaban that however much Red Khamet wanted to win, he wanted a *clear* win. He valued his reputation. The pearl lost value if he was dogged by rumors he'd got it unfairly.

"Where's Old Jalid?" he asked. "I thought I saw him."

"He's here," said someone at the back of the crowd.

"He knows the bones better than anyone," said Red Khamet. "We'll hear what he has to say. Have him brought forth."

A few moments later, a boy appeared, leading an elderly fellow leaning on a cane. The old man was thin and frail and walked unsteadily but Red Khamet's gang respectfully parted for him.

"Greetings, revered Jalid," said Red Khamet.

"Greetings, Red Khamet," responded Old Jalid in a quavery voice.

"You were gaming with the bones when most of us were unborn. You know every rule and every way to play. Will you settle a question for us?"

"I've played with the bones sixty-nine years," said Old Jalid in slow, formal tones, like a soldier recalling his battles. I've played on half the ships between here and Greece, and on some now at the bottom of the sea. If your question has an answer, I'll know it. Speak."

"One cube lies within the circle. One cube lies on the line itself. Together, they make seven. Is the one on the line to be allowed or not?"

"Is the cube *on* the line or does it only touch the line? And if it touches the line, is it mostly inside or outside the circle?"

Artaban considered this a strange question from someone who only had to look and see for himself. Then the torchlight flickered on the wrinkled face and he saw Old Jalid's milky, unfocused eyes. Blind! A blind man was to decide the matter. A blind man would pronounce if his pearl and Ismail's hand were forfeit! Truly, could things become any more upside-down?

"It is smack on the line," said Red Khamet. "If the line was a blade, it would cut the cube in half."

"Then it is both inside the circle *and* outside the circle," said Old Jalid. Artaban reflected that such a gift for riddling and lofty paradox was equaled only by some of the highest and windiest priests in his order. "It can't be both," he blurted.

Old Jalid turned his head in Artaban's direction. "Who speaks?" he asked.

"My opponent," said Red Khamet. "He is Artaban the Mage, a priest of Zoroaster."

Old Jalid made a gargling sound in his throat and Artaban realized he was laughing. "A mage *and* a priest of the Sun God?" he said. "Truly, do men of such wisdom and learning stoop to play so humble a sport?" The crowd tittered.

"He is new to the bones," said Red Khamet, "but the stakes are high."

"Well, they may be high or they may be low but my answer is the same," wheezed Old Jalid. "The cube is both inside the line and outside the circle."

The crowd began to murmur, returning to old arguments. Old Jalid raised his high voice. "*However*, since a thing cannot be two places at once, the cube is *neither* inside the circle *nor* outside it." Artaban suppressed a sigh. Truly, Old Jalid had missed his calling. He would have made a fine theology teacher.

"*Therefore*," continued Old Jalid. He paused until every voice in the crowd was silent. "The cube is fairly disputed and since a fair dispute may be argued fairly by both sides, the matter is beyond resolution." The crowd waited to hear his conclusion but apparently that was it. He said nothing more, a slight smile on his lips, perhaps reflecting satisfaction at his perfect wisdom. He turned to go and the baffled crowd opened for him.

"But what do we *do?*" said Red Khamet in frustration.

"Roll again," said Old Jalid over his shoulder.

Red Khamet sighed and turned to Artaban. "That's settled then. This round don't count. If you will, Mage, next time you toss, stay *off* the line."

It was a weak joke but the crowd laughed cheerfully. The tension temporarily broken, betting quickly resumed. Red Khamet kissed the bones, shook the cup and tossed. They came up four and five. "Nine," he muttered, handing the cup to Artaban.

Artaban dropped the bones in the cup, carefully held it just over the middle of the circle and tipped it. One showed five and the other six. Eleven. Artaban was about to hand the cup back to Red Khamet when cries of joy and disgust rose from the spectators.

"Eleven!"

"The Mage did it!"

"By Horus, he did!"

"Game's over!"

Artaban looked again at the cubes. *Eleven.* He'd thrown eleven. He'd *won.*

Red Khamet glowered at Artaban, then turned to Ismail's guards. "Let him go." The two released his arms. Ismail, trembling, gripped his right wrist with his left hand, as if to assure himself he still had it.

"He's saved your miserable hand, cheat," said Red Khamet. "Get out of here and stay away if you want to keep it." Ismail pushed through the crowd and quickly vanished.

Artaban and Red Khamet got to their feet and dusted off their clothes. Red Khamet held out his hand. "Congratulations, Mage." They shook. "Sometimes Miss Luck smiles on those with nerve. You're a better friend than that dog deserves. And now you're a friend of Red Khamet. May the Sun God smile on you."

"You're a fair man, hard but fair," replied Artaban. "May he smile on Red Khamet as well." He turned and stepped out of the alley into the street. A few steps later, he realized his mouth was dry and his knees shaky. There was a stand down the street that served fruit drinks. It usually had a free chair. He could sit there and calm his nerves.

ARTABAN headed for the stand. A close thing! Never would he take such a risk again. Not for anyone. Not for... something strange was going on around him. People were turning to stare. Why? What was amiss? Then he caught snatches of what they were saying to each other.

"Is that him?"

"That's him."

"He's the one."

"Beat Red Khamet at the bones."

"Bet a pearl to save his servant."

"Not just any pearl, biggest pearl in the world!"

"And not for his servant, for one who only used to be."

Artaban smiled. Word seemed to be spreading, and fast. He'd acquired a reputation, a kind of fame, at least in this part of Alexandria and at least for tonight.

A tall man with broad shoulders approached him. "Master, if you are in need of a new servant, consider this one if you will. I am experienced. I'm honest. I don't gamble or drink."

"Thank you, no," said Artaban quietly but firmly, walking on. He hadn't gone a block when another did the same. A few steps further and another appeared. He shook his head. So much for a quiet evening. He'd have no peace, not tonight. He turned and headed back toward his inn.

After several blocks, he'd apparently outpaced his reputation. People no longer stared and no one had approached him in the last few minutes. Then he heard footsteps. He would have walked faster but a great weariness had overtaken him.

"Master," a voice said.

He knew that voice. He found the strength to walk a little faster.

"Master," a hand grabbed at his sleeve. He shook it off.

Ismail appeared at his side, matching his stride. "Master, twice you've—"

"Don't call me, Master," said Artaban coldly. "You don't serve me."

"But I served you well when I served you. Let me again."

"You're a free man. Stay a free man or find some other master, but leave me in peace."

"How can I leave you when I owe you my life, twice now?"

"Would that I'd left you on the road to Borsippa! I'd still have my ruby and not risked my pearl."

"And you'd still have your sapphire, for because of me you got to Bethlehem days faster than you would have on your own. You would have missed the massacre. The baby you saved would be dead and when you came you might have found a town that would not even speak of the family that brought such grief. Who can say what might have been? I know this much for certain. If not for you, I would have lost this hand and likely my life. You have need of a servant. Let it be me."

"No. Has your mother been troubling your sleep again?"

"Mama's not been back, bless her. Give me a trial. Three days, no more. You'll wonder how you got on without me."

"So far, I've gotten on fine without you. I make my own tea. A washerwoman does my clothes. I eat at the inn. And I have all the solitude I want. Besides, I thought you couldn't serve a man bound to throw his life away on a delusion."

"That was the judgment of one who presumed to be your friend."

"And now you're not my friend?"

"A true servant is always a servant before a friend. I forgot that. What you do with your life is for you to decide. My sole concern will be to see to whatever you need. And to follow wherever you go."

"I need no one to follow me. My destiny—my folly, my 'lunacy'—is mine only. I ask no one to share it. I want no one's help."

"Everyone needs someone's help one time or another, Master, but let that pass. At least you *know* your destiny, whether it's faith or folly. Most men don't. I didn't... until tonight."

"And what is that, besides a meal, a woman or someone new to gull?"

"To serve you, that is my destiny."

Artaban stopped and turned, speechless. Ismail stared at him with tears in his eyes. He was used to Ismail's tears. He'd seem them often. The man was not only sentimental and given to display but when necessary he could make them spout at will. No, it wasn't the tears that surprised Artaban. It was Ismail's voice, his quiet tone of conviction. "To serve me?"

"To the end of my days, wherever you go."

Such a pledge made Artaban uncomfortable, not because he doubted it but because he thought it might be genuine, and not stemming from relief and gratitude, but from something deeper, the kind of bond that connected brothers. No, deeper than that, the kind of devotion felt by husbands and wives. No, still deeper, the kind of fervor worshippers gave to their gods, even when those gods were no more than stone idols.

Well, he had no need of a brother or a partner and he was not about to become anyone's idol. "Ismail, I did what I did knowing the risk, just as I did at Borsippa. You owe me nothing. Go and spend your life how you will, but you will not spend it serving me."

He began to walk again. The inn was only a little distance now. Ismail kept pace. "Mayhap I owe you nothing. Mayhap I owe you everything. That's no matter for that's not why I want to serve you."

Artaban stopped again. "Then why?"

Ismail ran his hand through his hair. "It's hard to explain, but... when I woke up in the morning, I knew what I had to do, which was whatever you needed for that day. I had a *purpose*, if you will, and that was worth passing up a game of the bones or an easy chance to separate a man from his purse. You're a good man, Master. To serve you was an easy thing. But now I think you're more than that. I think you're a great man. To serve you, that's an honor."

"A great man?" said Artaban in astonishment. "I've done nothing great!"

"You've saved two lives that I know of—mine and the babe's—and I've seen you doctor other people–that fellow with the toothache, the woman who was afraid she'd lose her baby. They didn't ask you, didn't even know to ask you. You just helped them on your own. I expect you've been doing that a long time. And you know other things, the stars for example, how they govern our lives. You can explain dreams. The candle maker's daughter, the one who was sick with fear on account she kept dreaming of snakes? You spent a whole morning with her, got her to understand a dream snake might be a *good* thing, could mean a life change."

"These are the things every man owes his fellow man. They are not great deeds."

"Maybe, maybe not, though I think Isaac and his wife might have a different view of it. Suppose you're not a great man, you still have greatness in you. If the moment comes, you'll be worthy of it. Now Herod, he sits on a throne but that doesn't make him a great man. He's a small, mean-spirited man who's made his throne and Judea smaller and meaner."

Artaban sighed. "The highborn may have low natures. You're right there, but learning and kind deeds do not make for a great man. That's *your* folly, Ismail, and if I argue with you more, I'm in peril of coming to share it. Here is the inn and here is where we part. I have no need of a servant, however much you have need of a master. I hope you find one worthy of you, for you have many fine qualities. Goodnight. Go your way, and though I don't, as some think, worship 'the Sun God,' I hope the sun smiles kindly on you."

He held out his hand, his anger had faded. Ismail took it but dropped to one knee and kissed the back of it. "I won't shake, Master, for I'm not your equal. I'm your servant, now and for always, want me or not."

Artaban withdrew his hand and went into the inn, feeling unsettled, and went to bed soon after. That night he dreamed he was hurrying through a twisty, narrow lane. It was night and only a bit of moonlight to go by. Not far off, dark figures were hurrying toward him. He felt something momentous was about to happen, perhaps the end of his quest, but he and the figures began to move slower and slower. It was taking forever to reach them. Then the scene faded and broke apart into a familiar jumble of dream images. Try as he might, he could not get back to the narrow lane. In the morning he woke and pondered his dream but the meaning eluded him.

He dressed and opened the door of his room to go down for breakfast. Ismail was curled up on the floor in front of it, sound asleep. Artaban poked him with his foot and he promptly woke. "Is this where you spent the night?" he asked with a mixture of annoyance and dismay.

"It is," Ismail answered with a yawn.

"A hard bed."

"I've slept on harder. Where are we bound today, Master?"

"I'm not your master, and *I'm* bound for breakfast."

"Fine. There's a lady who makes meat pies only two blocks away. I'll gobble one and be back before you've finished."

"Take your time. *I* have much to do today, including finding a ship bound for Athens. I'm booking passage for one."

"I worked as a sea cook once. Ships are always in need of a good cook. I'll work off my fare that way."

Artaban shook his head and went down to breakfast. Ismail vanished but, as promised, was back before his porridge was cold. He accompanied Artaban to the pier and though the Mage pointedly ignored him, was taken as his servant by almost all they met. Artaban finally settled on a sturdy freighter called *Calypso's Daughter*, sailing at high tide two mornings hence. When he left, Ismail stayed behind to chat with the boatswain and mate.

 Artaban saw him no more that day but found him sleeping in the hall the next morning. Artaban poked him and he scrambled up. "Meet the new cook of *Calypso's Daughter*," he grinned.

# Chapter Fourteen

## The Philosophers of Athens

TO THE eye, Athens was a splendid town of stately columned buildings, cool public baths and magnificent statuary. To the ear, it was a constant, buzzing murmur of conversation, contention, discussion, proclamation, prediction, reflection, rumination and just plain chatter. The Athenians loved to talk and in their minds, they did it better than anyone.

Mostly, it was the men who talked, or at least talked in the open. Athenian women probably talked as much as their men but they did it at home or the market and likely they talked of banal, common things like children and meals and sewing and laundry and so on.

Men, on the other hand, gathered in clumps in the baths or squares or taverns or simply wandered the city. Unlike the women, they talked of serious, important matters, principally ideas. They talked of all sorts of ideas, those concerning politics and history and nature and art and the gods and philosophy and even loftier, more abstract topics. In fact, the more abstract an idea, the less it concerned gross matters such as money or food or children, the more it was valued and the greater the stature of the talker.

Artaban took pleasure in ideas and spirited debate but even he wearied of the town's inexhaustible appetite for speculations and theories that transcended earthly bonds and seemed to float, cloudlike, on the thermals that rose wherever Athenians gathered to talk, talk, talk.

Ismail was with him, of course, since it had become obvious Artaban could not detach himself from a man determined to serve him whether he was paid or not. Besides, he *was* useful and seemed genuine in his vow to give up gaming and stealing.

The two of them quizzed the philosophical men of Athens, who predictably knew nothing of a humble Jewish family newly arrived from Egypt or elsewhere. After several days they gave up on the philosophers and went to the markets where the women and shopkeepers of Athens provided them with gossip and news about the city's great and small and in between but, alas, nothing about Joseph and his family.

Thus two weeks passed. Ismail rose one morning to discover his master already up, sitting at the table writing on a parchment. He made tea and when he served it, Artaban bid him sit. "There are other Greek cities and towns to visit, and I intend to visit all of any size. You will not be with me, for I'm sending you to Ecbatana. I want you to go to my house and give this letter to my steward, Jabar."

"What is in the letter, Master?"

"It tells him to sell my house and belongings, to pay pensions to my longtime servants and a year's wages to all others, various other provisions."

Ismail couldn't hide his dismay. "You're selling your home? Where will you live?"

Artaban pointing out the window, which looked onto the street, already crowded with traffic, people traveling by foot and horse and wagon to other parts of the city or perhaps to other cities. "*That* is my home, the road, at least for now and the foreseeable future. Wherever Joseph and his family have gone, it's evident they will not be easily found. This quest is likely to take the rest of the year and I would not be surprised if it takes most of next year, maybe another. However long it takes, we need money to live on. I won't be returning to Ecbatana in any case. I could not live there without daily seeing things that reminded me of Rasha. The grief would be too great. When the child has been found, there will be money left to find a dwelling closer to him. As he grows, he'll need a teacher and I would like to be that teacher. And too, I hope to write a chronicle of his life and doings."

"What do you want me to do, besides convey the letter?"

"You'll stay at my house until everything has been arranged. It will take a while, probably several months. There'll be much to do and I'm sure Jabar will make use of you. When all is done, return here with the money. A servant named Hakim will ride back with you. He's an experienced traveler and one-time soldier. I don't doubt your discretion but both you and my gold will be safer in his company."

"Where will you be?"

"Somewhere else, I'm sure, but I'll make this inn my base. The innkeeper knows how to read and write. I'll send him letters from time to time on my whereabouts and how to reach me. Once you and Hakim get to Athens, his duty is done and he can return to

Ecbatana. Have the innkeeper contact me and wait here. I hope by then I'll have some news of the family, however small, and we'll plan our next steps.

"As you say, Master. Though I don't like the idea of being away from you so long."

Artaban smiled and clapped his servant on the shoulder. "Our roads will part for a while but they'll join again. You've been with me on this quest from the beginning, Ismail. I want you there when it's done. After we find the boy we'll look for a modest dwelling, one with a decent kitchen so you can cook. Maybe there'll be land for a garden. We could grow vegetables."

"And perhaps a small pen for goats? And a roost for fowl? Vegetables go better with meat and eggs."

Artaban smiled. "Why not? A settled life. That's something to look forward to." His smile faded and he was silent for a moment. "I had planned to have such a life with Rasha back in Ecbatana, surrounded by children, but the One, who sets all things in motion and ends our days, decided that was not to be." He turned to his servant. "Ismail, who have you loved in your life?"

"I've loved many women for a while, but never anyone so much I wanted to spend my life with her. You're lucky there, Master."

"Lucky? I lost her without ever sharing a bed with her."

"Yes, but the memory of her still warms you, doesn't it?"

"That's true. When I think of her, I feel a gladness in my heart."

"That you feel for no other?"

"No, none. You loved your mother though, didn't you?"

"That I did. And she loved me, loved me more than anyone else in my miserable life. She was a fierce old woman but I knew no matter how bad I became, Mama would always love me. She was always after me to settle down."

"Well, if the One permits, perhaps this time next year, or the year after, we will settle down. Someday this quest will end and when it does, we'll turn the page and begin a new chapter in our lives, you and I, a couple of old bachelors."

# Chapter Fifteen

## The Innkeeper

THE BEDS at Sailors Inn had clean sheets and mattresses stuffed with fresh straw and the chamber pots were emptied daily. Meals were hot and tasty and the innkeeper didn't water the ale. The inn's stable was clean, the stable roof free of leaks and it wasn't uncommon to find travelers sharing quarters there with their horses, for Sailors Inn was one of the most popular in Alexandria and when there were no rooms, the proprietor would let latecomers bed down for three pennies each.

The innkeeper was a stout, bald man in early middle-age and though it had been years since he'd sported a bright shock of crimson hair, everyone still called him Red Khamet. When his son knocked at his door, he was undressing for bed, trying to make as little noise as possible, for his wife was already asleep. Jaleh was in her seventh month and woke easily and if she did, inclined to be cranky.

Young Khamet was his eldest, thirteen, and the abundant hair on his head was bright as a flame. "What is it?" said his father a little irritably. It had been a long day.

"Late travelers, two," said the boy. "I put them in the stable."

"So?"

"So one of them asked about you."

"So?" Red Khamet had a wide reputation from his seafaring days and that had only grown since opening the inn a dozen years back. It was a rare day when at least one guest didn't know him from a previous stay or long ago voyage.

"Nothing more. He said he would look for you tomorrow. One thing strange though."

"What's that?" said Red Khamet with growing impatience. The hall was cold and the draft threatened to blow out his candle.

"He wished me a happy birthday."

"What's strange about that? Yesterday *was* your birthday."

"Yes but how did he know?"

Red Khamet's eyes went wide. "These travelers, what did they look like?"

"Tall man and his servant. He's older than you, hair turning silver, talked like he was educated. He spoke to me in Egyptian but he and his servant talked Greek."

"And the servant, what about him?"

"Younger than the other, short and plump, homeliest man I've ever seen."

"Horus have mercy!" declared Red Khamet. "And you put them in the *stable?*"

"We're filled, Papa. Nowhere to put them, except the King's Suite." The King's Suite was two spacious rooms with carpets and a view of the port, reserved for wealthy merchants and their wives.

"Then that's where we'll put them," said Red Khamet, pulling on his pants.

"Papa, they don't look like they can afford it."

"Afford it? You think I'd *charge* such a man?"

"What is it?" complained Jaleh groggily.

"Nothing, my sweet," soothed Red Khamet. "Nothing you need worry about. Go back to sleep." He grabbed his shoes and shirt and slipped into the hall. "Come along," he told his son. "Let's move them before they get settled."

Red Khamet had the boy light a lantern while he finished dressing and they walked across the yard to the stable. He rapped at the door and Nadim, the stable hand, let them inside.

"A thousand pardons, my old friends!" Red Khamet declared loudly to the two travelers, who were about to bed down in a pile of straw.

They turned to him and smiled, the tall man broadly, the servant tentatively. "Greetings, Red Khamet," he said. "We didn't want to wake you."

"As if I wouldn't want to welcome Artaban the Mage any time of the day or night!" said Red Khamet, embracing him heartily. He turned to the servant. "Ismail! You scoundrel, still have your hand, I see! Give it to me! Come on, you know all's forgiven."

Ismail held out his hand hesitantly and Red Khamet seized and shook it like he was working a water pump. He turned to Artaban and gestured at the boy. "You've met my son, Young Khamet. Forgive him for not knowing you. He wasn't so tall the last time you were here."

"If I recall, he barely came to his father's waist," said Artaban. "You've grown, lad, and your hair is even redder." He shook hands with the boy, who smiled self-consciously. Strangers were always telling him how much he'd grown.

Red Khamet and his son quickly gathered the pair's belongings and escorted them to the inn. When Artaban saw where they were to be lodged, he protested. "This is much too fine for us. All we require is—"

"Nothing is too fine for you, my friend," said Red Khamet, lighting candles. "It's the only free room tonight, so you'll have to put up with the pillows and carpets. Tomorrow, if you prefer, I'll switch you to something more modest."

He gazed at the two travelers. How long ago was that game of bones? Fifteen years? They'd aged. Well, so had he and Jaleh but then they saw each other everyday, so you didn't notice. It had been at least five years since the Mage's last visit. The toil of constant travel had worn him down. He remembered how Artaban had looked when first they'd met that night outside Hama's tavern, tall and elegant in a fine robe of purple linen, a turban of spotless white silk wrapped about his head. He was still tall but now slightly stooped and while his attire was respectable, you'd not call it elegant. His robe was a dull brown, worn and discreetly patched. His beard was neatly trimmed but flecked with gray hairs. Ismail looked much the same, a little fatter, balding on top with maybe a few extra lines in his comical face.

"Are the two of you hungry?" he asked.

"No, just tired," said Artaban. "Thank you for your hospitality, Red Khamet."

"You're ever welcome at Sailors Inn, both of you." He bowed to them, his son doing likewise, and they departed.

"Papa, who are they?" asked Young Khamet as they went down the hallway.

"Friends, good friends of mine and your mother's. I'm sure to catch it in the morning when she finds I didn't tell her."

"Friends from your sailor days? He doesn't look like a sailor."

"He's not. His name is Artaban the Mage."

Red Khamet led his son into the kitchen and found a pear, which he sliced in quarters and put on a plate. "I'm hungry," he said. "And you *always* are." He poured two glasses of milk and they went into the dark and vacant dining room.

"What's a Mage?"

"A priest of Zoroaster."

"The Sun God?"

"Zoroaster was the Sun God's prophet, but yes, that one. He's an educated man, can read and write, speaks more languages than fingers on your hands. Knows the stars. He has a magic looker that brings them near. If you ask, he'll let you put it to your eye some night. He loves to explain things."

"How did you meet him?"

Red Khamet smiled and shook his head. "Him and me, we played at the bones once."

"The bones? Him?"

"Him. He'd never played before but he bet a pearl to keep his servant out of trouble."

"What kind of trouble?"

"Trouble with *me* and don't ask more because that was in my roving days, before I met your mother." He smiled. "Before I got tamed, you might say. Anyway he won. The two of them show up in Alexandria every few years."

"The King's Suite! He must be a great friend of yours."

"He is. Yours too. If not for him, you wouldn't be here. Likely not your mother neither."

"What do you mean?"

"They were here the night you were born. That was about a year after I'd opened the inn. It was much smaller then, just six rooms. They were on their way from Syria, or *to* Syria, I can't recall which. When they heard about the inn, they put up here. It was your time but somehow you'd gotten turned around inside."

"Turned around?"

"You were coming out the wrong way, or rather you *weren't* – coming out, I mean. Your grandmother and aunt were here and they thought they could handle matters. Naleh had midwifed more than a few women. But she'd never come up against this before. He heard your mother, well, the whole inn heard your mother! Women make a lot of noise when they're birthing, but he could tell something was wrong. He came to me and said he might be able to help. I knew he could doctor, so I told them. By then they were desperate, so they let him have a look. I wasn't there—I mean, in the room—but they said it was touch and go. In the end, he got you out and stopped her bleeding. That was close too. Afterwards, when I saw how pale she was, I don't mind telling you I went pale myself. He'd gone into another room with your aunt to wash you off. I found him, tears in my eyes, and got on my knees and kissed his hand, blood and all. Told him whenever he was in Alexandria to come to Sailors Inn. There'd always be a room for him and Ismail, no charge."

Young Khamet was wide-eyed. He'd never heard this story before. "So that's how he knew my birthday."

Red Khamet nodded. "The next day he did your star chart. Gave it to us and said the signs were auspicious for you."

Young Khamet grinned. "Auspicious how?"

"Said you've have your mother's wits and your father's nerve, my hair too." He ran his head across his smooth pate. "*Haw!* Let's hope you keep yours longer."

"What else did he say?"

"Said you'd be good with numbers but to keep you away from the sea, for you weren't born for sailing. Your mother was glad to hear that, for women look on the ocean as the siren that pulls their men and boys away. Born for it or not, we need you here. This will be *your* place someday."

"The Mage, where is he from?"

"Persia once upon a time but his home has been the road since I've known him. Never in one place long. He's searching, you see."

"Searching for what?"

Red Khamet's brows furrowed. "That's harder to explain. For a certain child, though he'd be… um, well, closer to fifteen now, almost a man."

"Who is he? Is he Artaban's son?"

"No, it's not that. The child was born under a star. Prophecies said someday the boy would rule, or that's what he's told me"

"Rule what?"

"*That* I'm not so sure about, Judea maybe. That's where he was born."

"Why would a Persian care who rules Judea?"

"You've got me there. Something special about this one, not just an ordinary king. If you ask him, he can tell you better."

"And he was born under a star?"

"So the Mage says."

"Which star?"

"A bright one that rose in the East. It's gone now."

"Gone! Papa, the stars are *always* here. They don't come and go."

"Some do. Wandering stars, they're called. This was one such. I saw it myself. Shone brighter than any other for a few months, then it faded and vanished. Artaban, when he got to where the boy was born, the family had already gone, fled. They were running from Herod."

"Who's Herod"

"Dead now, but back then he was king of Judea. He'd heard the same prophecies, worried about his throne. Anyway Artaban set out after the babe, been looking for him ever since."

"For how long did you say?"

"Well, when we met he'd been on the trail for the better part of six months. You came along a couple of years later. So fifteen years, more or less."

Young Khamet looked incredulous. "*Fifteen years?*"

"Aye. He's a determined man."

"What will he do if he finds this child?"

"Give him a pearl."

"A pearl?"

"Aye, the same one we gambled for. It's his gift to the child."

"Papa, forgive me, I know he's your friend, but he doesn't sound right in the head."

Red Khamet frowned. "That's not for you or me to say, and don't speak of it again unless you want your face slapped. He's a friend of this family. He's always welcome here, as long as he wants to stay, no charge for food or lodging."

"All right, Papa. I'm sorry."

"That's all right. They won't stay long. They never do. They'll spend the next few days asking around, looking for a Jewish family with an eldest son that stands out." Red Khamet chortled. "*Haw!* What would any mother or father say about their eldest? 'Stand out? I should say our boy does!' He's a man who doesn't give up, is Artaban. A good thing, for this task of his is a long one."

He reached across the table and tousled his son's hair. "Wash the glass and plate, then go to bed. It'll be day all too soon. Mouths to feed, rooms to clean, money to be made and paid."

He took his candle and made his way upstairs. Sometimes he missed his roving days, especially when an old mate dropped by and they had an ale and a few laughs. Most of the time, though, he was glad to be out of it, to sleep in the same bed every night beside the same woman, to wake in the morning and greet his children. Innkeeping was hard work, don't let anyone tell you otherwise. but a family made all of it worthwhile. He couldn't imagine life without Jaleh and the children.

What, he wondered, kept Artaban going? No home, no wife, no family but Ismail, who Red Khamet had to admit, was as devoted to him as any wife. He didn't doubt Artaban loved him after a fashion but still, the man wasn't kin. As to the quest, it was hopeless of course. Artaban would never find this infant who had become a child and then a boy and now a youth and someday a man. Never.

Red Khamet let himself in his bedroom and blew out the candle. Not for him to judge the Mage or his quest. Young Khamet had the right of it, though. Artaban was more than a bit touched, though in his obsession there was a kind of magnificent madness. And what if someday he *did* find who he sought?

Red Khamet sighed as he crawled into bed next to Jaleh. Well, if that day ever came, he hoped that one was worthy of the quest. If it was to be, may it come soon.

# Chapter Sixteen

## The Galilean

FROM Egypt, Artaban and Ismail traveled to Judea and then to Syria and on to Thrace and then Greece, then across the sea back to Egypt. The years passed and the cities and towns came and went and came back: Alexandria, Jerusalem, Damascus, Antioch, Byzantium, Thesalonica, Athens, Corinth and back to Alexandria, then on to Jerusalem once more and so on until they were back again in Alexandria, where Young Khamet, now a grown man and father of three, ran Sailors Inn, his father having died of a fever.

They were welcome there, of course, just as they'd ever been. This time they stayed for several months while the two replenished Artaban's thinning purse by working, Ismail as a cook and Artaban as a doctor and dentist and caster of horoscopes.

At length they traveled on. In thirty years of searching, they had become familiar figures in the towns they visited: a tall, white-bearded old man in a tattered robe and his fat, homely servant. They were treated with respect but afterwards there was often a smile and a shaking of the head. To those who recognized him but didn't know him, Artaban went by different names. Many called him "the Mage," in respect of his learning and healing skills. Sometimes he was called the "boy seeker," though it had been long since he'd sought a boy. Less kindly, others knew him as the "wandering loon."

Ismail was simply called the "servant," sometimes the "ugly one." He was seldom away from his master's side. From time to time in the street he and Artaban would pass a clutch of men playing at bones and his eyes would flick to the game with a hint of nostalgia. It had been more than thirty years since he'd last gambled. Nor in that time had he stolen a purse (though there were occasions when he was sore tempted), or lifted a glass of ale or wine or spirits to his lips. His master's cause was the boy born under the star. Ismail's cause was his master. Nothing else mattered.

THEY had been in Jerusalem only a day when they first heard of the raising at Bethany. The story was that a woman's brother was seriously ill and she had sent word to a traveling healer with a growing reputation. The brother worsened and died before he arrived. When he did, four days later, the woman rebuked him. The healer went to the tomb and called for the dead man to come forth. The woman and her family rolled their eyes; some tittered. Their derision turned to open-mouthed astonishment when Lazarus stumbled into the daylight, alive and fully restored.

Artaban was accustomed to this sort of tale. They were in the marketplace, at a date seller's stall, and the man telling it had a rapt audience. As it turned out, he had not actually been there himself, but the wife of a good friend had been and she was wholly reliable.

"This healer, what is he called?" Artaban asked.

"He's called Jesus," said the speaker. "He's coming here."

"To Jerusalem?"

"Yes."

"When?"

"Soon, old one. Soon, I hear. Why? Are you hoping he will raise you if you die beforehand?"

The crowd at the stall laughed. Artaban bristled and left. "I weary of these tales of miracle makers," he told Ismail. "Not a land that we've been in that doesn't have such stories, but they always happen in some *other* town. The lame walk. The blind see. And now the dead come forth! No one has ever seen them do it but they know someone who *has*. I have no small skill as a healer myself. That fellow with the useless arm? You saw me give him back use of it."

"I did indeed, Master, but it was no miracle. It was your herbs and ointment and it took a week."

"Exactly! It was medicine, not a miracle. No one, *no one*, Ismail, can bring back the dead." They walked on. Artaban's mood did not improve. "'Old one,' he called me."

"People today have no respect," said Ismail.

"That fat sluggard! I could have walked his legs off."

"You could indeed, Master. Where do we go now?"

"Jericho. The fellow at the tavern spoke of a Galilean who's gotten crowds with his teaching. He said there was a couple in Jericho who'd heard him."

"Shall I find us a pair of camels?"

"Yes, from someone who will buy them back when we return. I'm going to the inn. We'll leave in the morning."

"HE'S THE son of a carpenter," said Abraham, a portly man who was himself a carpenter and came out of his Jericho workshop to talk with Artaban. "But I don't think the Galilean's done any carpentry himself. Soft hands." He displayed his own calloused hands. "Well-spoken though. Talks like yourself, sir. Educated, I mean."

"Voice like music," said his wife Susannah. "I'm one who drifts off when our rabbi talks but he held me, just *held* me, with his words."

"What did he talk about?" asked Artaban. They were sitting outside, under the shade of a large fig tree, drinking fruit juice Susannah had served.

"About God," said Susannah, "but not like our rabbi. Doesn't talk so much about the Law."

"More about mercy," said Abraham.

"Mercy?"

"Mercy and forgiving. Says God forgives us. All we have to do is ask. No matter how much we've sinned, He forgives."

"So we should do the same," said Susannah. "Said it's wrong to store up anger against someone, even if it's justified. The way he explained, I saw things in a new light. I'd been angry with Sarah—that's my sister—for six years, on account of she... well, I don't need to go into all that. So the first thing I did when we got home was to go to her house and hug her, 'It's all right, Sarah,' I said. "What's past is past.'

Susannah laughed. "She was just stunned. Had to sit down, on account of I, well, I guess I'm what you might call stubborn. She looked at me, tears in her eyes, and said, 'Susannah, I didn't think I'd ever hear those words.' I said, 'Well, now you have. You want to thank someone, thank a man named Jesus."

Artaban and Ismail exchanged glances. "That's the Galilean?" said Artaban. "Jesus?"

"Yes."

"The same one who raised a dead man?"

"Hadn't heard that," said Abraham. "But he made a man who couldn't use his legs walk again."

"That's right," agreed Susannah.

"He spoke of this?"

"No. We saw it."

"You *saw* it?"

"We did," said Abraham. "While he was talking, a family came in carrying the old granddad. Hadn't walked in years, they said. So Jesus touched his legs, told him to get up and he got right up."

"Well, not right up," said Susannah. "Took him a couple of minutes. He was pretty shaky, leaned on his son. Got better at it and when they left he was walking on his own."

Artaban glanced at Ismail. It wasn't unknown for fake healers to use foils. "Did you know this man, the one who walked?"

"We didn't but some others did," said Abraham. "They were coming up to him and hugging and kissing. Quite a scene it was. Only one not excited was Jesus, acted like he did this all the time. Maybe he does."

"Did he do any other healings?"

"No, but afterwards, a young woman with child came up and asked for his blessing," said Abraham. "He gave it and said, 'You will have a daughter. Call her Mary, for that is my mother's name.'"

"And then he made a little joke," said Susannah. "He said, 'I hope you give birth in your own house, with your husband and sisters around you. When I was born my companions were livestock.'" She laughed at the memory.

"Livestock?"

"Yes. He said his parents were traveling but the inns were full, so someone let them stay in a stable."

"What town? Did he say?"

"He did," said Abraham, scratching his jaw. He turned to his wife. "Bethel, was it?"

"No, Bethlehem."

"Bethlehem. That's right."

"What about his father? Did he mention him?"

"Well, that's a little confusing," Abraham replied. "He said he had *two* fathers. The one who brought him up wasn't his natural father but he was strong and kind. His name was Joseph."

"Joseph!" said Ismail.

"Common enough name," said Abraham, a little perplexed at the servant's exclamation. "But his other father, he didn't talk about him." He rose. "I have to get back to work. That's all we can tell you about the Galilean, but if you want to know more you can go to Jerusalem and ask him yourself."

Artaban and Ismail rose. "We'd heard he was coming."

"He's already come," said Susanna. "My brother Malachi told me yesterday. He was in Jerusalem near the gate when Jesus came in with his people. Made quite a stir. Seems a lot of people know about him."

"Thanks to both of you," said Artaban. He clasped their hands warmly.

"Good luck," said Abraham. "Next time you're in Jericho, come by and tell us what you make of him."

They mounted their camels and set off a brisk trot. Jerusalem was two days off and it was already late afternoon. "Do you think he could be the one?" said Ismail.

"He might be," said Artaban, trying to keep the excitement out of his voice. "They said he's in his early thirties so he's the right age. We'll know more when we find him."

"After all these years..." said Ismail. "Hard to believe we've found him."

"We haven't, not yet. We've had other disappointments, old friend. Let's not pin all our hopes on this Jesus yet."


IT WAS the week of Passover and Jerusalem was crowded with those who had come to observe the festival. The Inn of the Lamb, which they'd left for Jericho, was filled, so they walked through the streets thick with visitors to Jacob's Inn. There were no rooms there either but they lingered in the common room, where people were talking about how the Galilean had entered Jerusalem.

"He rode a donkey," said an old man with the look of a scholar. "The crowd loved it, but I heard it riled the priests."

"Why is that?" asked Artaban.

"Well, it has to do with custom," the scholar explained. "Warrior kings, when they enter a town, they ride chariots or chargers, you know, show how mighty they are. But a king who rides a donkey comes in peace. Solomon, the day he was made king, he rode a donkey."

"Has Jesus said he's king?"

"Not that I've heard but some do. The priests, you can see how Caiaphas and his ilk would think he's putting on airs."

"From healer to teacher to king," Artaban said to Ismail when they left. "That's a dangerous game and not just with the priesthood. If Herod's son Antipas hears of this, he won't like it either."

There were no rooms to be had at the Inn of the White Horse, but the air was buzzing with what the Galilean had done at the Temple.

"He knocked over the tables of the moneychangers," said a stout woman. "Chased them out with a rope whip." She laughed. "He's not a big man, just ordinary. But, oh my, he was fierce! You should have seen them run!"

"You saw this?" said Artaban.

"With my own eyes," said the woman, grinning and dabbing at her eyes, which had watered with her merriment. "He told them, 'You've set up a thieves' den in my father's house.' Oh my, never seen anything like it!"

"Those were his words, 'in my father's house?' What did he mean?"

"Well, you know, God is father of us all, isn't He?"

"You heard him yourself?"

"That I did."

"He said '*my* father?' Not 'our father?'"

"'My father' is what he said, but I expect he meant '*our*.' Just got excited."

"The moneychangers," said a small thin man with an oversized turban, "they'll be back tomorrow. Count on it."

"Well, then he'll throw 'em out again!" said the stout woman with a laugh.

"The priests won't like that," muttered a traveler from Shiloh. "The moneychangers pay a tithe to set up in the Temple."

"They're right about the priests," Ismail said as they made their way through the crowded streets. "They make a tidy income from the moneychangers. Bad enemies to have."

"No doubt," agreed Artaban. "But why did he say 'my father's house?'"

"Like the woman said, he was excited. Misspoke is all."

"Did he? Maybe. If he means to claim kingship, by what right? He's not Herod's son. Maybe he claims an older lineage."

"You mean David? Descended from King David?"

"I don't know what I mean," said Artaban, shaking his head. "I can't quite grasp it. I know this much, we must see this man ourselves."

# Chapter Seventeen

## The Pearl

THEY finally found shelter not at an inn but at the dwelling of a widow who let them rent a small back room. Her house was large and the other rooms were occupied by friends of her son Andrew, one of the band that traveled with Jesus. "Disciples," they called themselves. Artaban and Ismail stayed up late listening to the conversation, which centered around the doings of the Galilean and the anger he'd stirred among the priesthood. Eventually the two retired, resolving to find Jesus the next day.

It was still dark when they were wakened by raised voices elsewhere in the house. They followed the noise through the dark to a room bright with candles. Men, mostly young, crowded the space. Artaban saw faces from earlier in the evening but new ones as well. "He's been arrested!" one of them angrily told him.

"Jesus? By the Romans?"

"Soldiers, Chaim says."

"Soldiers but not Romans," said Levi, a tall young man with curly hair. "He and the disciples put up in the olive grove at the foot of the mount. I was on my way there when I saw soldiers coming from the grove. I ducked out of sight and they marched right by me, him in the middle. They were Temple guards, about a dozen or so. I followed at a distance. They took him to Caiaphas' palace."

"Caiaphas!" growled a thin, balding young man. "So the high priest is behind this."

"What about the disciples? Where are they?"

"They're scattered," said Levi. "In hiding."

"What is Jesus charged with?" asked Artaban.

"Heresy, I expect," said a broad-shoulder man with a dark beard. "Pack of lies!"

"They're afraid of him," said a man with a big nose.

"They want him dead," said another.

"They mean to stone him," said the balding one.

"We can't let them!"

"What can we do?" asked a plump fellow in the back of the room.

"Something, we have to do something!"

"And *now*, while there's time," said Levi fiercely.

"They'll probably keep him at the palace," said an older man. "At least until daylight when they can organize a trial."

"So-called, he doesn't have a chance."

"No, they'll convict him."

"Then stone him, all nice and legal."

"I've been to Caiaphas's palace," said a stocky man in a green robe. "It's not heavily guarded. We could get a bunch together and storm it."

"They'll send to Herod for help. The Romans will come."

"We can get inside and get him out before they get there," said Levi.

"Then what?"

"Hide him. Jerusalem is full of people friendly to Jesus. Wait until dark, then spirit him out of town."

"The guards might put up more of a fight than you expect."

"There's a better way," said a stout man well into middle age. "Caiaphas is too close-fisted to have proper Temple guards. They're just thugs, loyal to whoever puts coin in their hands. We could bribe them and get him out without a fight."

"Bribes are costly. How would we raise the money?"

"It's an idea but whatever we raise, it has to be quick," said Levi. "Everyone, go rouse your friends. Meet me at the palace of Caiaphas in an hour. If we don't have the money we'll storm the palace." A moment later he vanished out the door. The others dressed in haste.

Artaban and Ismail returned to their room. "Master, this may end badly," said Ismail gloomily.

"It may indeed," nodded Artaban. "They're neither soldiers nor organized. Even if they have the numbers, they'll have trouble overcoming a determined defense, whether the defenders are soldiers or thugs. And if they can't do it quickly, they'll be routed by the Romans."

"Even if they get inside," said Ismail. "the high priest may have Jesus killed before he lets him get away."

Artaban sat on the edge of his bed. "A bribe has the best chance of getting him out alive, I think, but they're not likely to raise enough, not in the middle of the night"

"To come so close," said Ismail in anguish. "I wanted to meet the man. I really did."

"And I wanted to give him my …" Artaban didn't finish his thought. He sat thoughtfully for a moment, then went to his money belt and unfastened a pocket. He took out a linen purse and from it removed his pearl. He held it in his palm. The candle flickered across its milky, lustrous surface and though it was large, the surrounding darkness made it seem even larger. It seemed to glow from its own inner light.

They silently admired its beauty for long moments, then Artaban shut his hand around it and stood. "I see it clearly now. *This* is my destiny."

"Destiny?" said Ismail.

Artaban turned to him. "This is why I came across you on the road to Borsippa so long ago, why I was delayed, why the others were gone when I got to the Temple of Fire. This is why we came late to Bethlehem, why for thirty-three years we have searched but never found him – until now. And *this* is why we were in Jericho when he arrived in Jerusalem."

"Why, Master?" asked Ismail, though he'd already guessed the answer.

"The One has held me back, kept me on his trail but never let me get too close because He knew this night would come, and he knew Jesus would have need of me… and the pearl."

"To buy his freedom from the palace guards?"

"Yes. Ismail, fate has put us here at a turning point in history. If Jesus dies, he will never claim his throne and the triumphs to come will never take place. On this pearl hinges the fate of the world."

"Then we must be quick."

Artaban pulled on his tunic and pants and wrapped the money belt around his waist. He slipped on his sandals, put on a robe and donned his turban. Finally he thrust his trusty blade in the belt. A moment later, the two men stepped out into the darkened streets to find their way to Caiaphas's palace. Dawn was yet an hour away and the streets were still and empty. Only a few vendors were up, trundling barrows of produce and goods on their way to set up their market stalls. The moon was high and it made their shadows long as they threaded their way through Jerusalem's cobbled lanes, no one to note their passing but stray dogs and slinking cats. Occasionally they would glimpse two or three young men talking loudly and hurrying in the same direction. *Please let us be in time,"* Artaban mumbled beneath his breath.

He paused at a tug on his cloak. Ismail pointed to a narrow alley. "A shortcut. I know it of old. We'll gain a few minutes."

They hurried through the winding alley, past the back doors of shops and dwellings, past heaps of refuse and scurrying rats. It led through an older part of the city where buildings were left in disrepair. More than once they passed roof tiles that had cracked and fallen.

A block distant they sighted dark forms as much in haste as themselves but coming through the alley toward them. A few moments later they made out four figures, two males and two females. Closer, they could see the females were bound by the wrists and led on a rope by a big man. A small one with a short whip followed after. "Silence, you two," he barked. "Or I'll give you cause for weeping!"

Another moment and the four were almost upon Artaban and Ismail. "Stand aside and let us pass," warned the big man. "We're in a hurry."

Artaban stopped but stayed where he was, he and Ismail blocking the alley. His voice was calm but stern. "Who are you and where are you taking these women?"

The little man drew himself up. "I'm Farbod the Moneylender and don't interfere if you want to stay out of trouble." He drew a parchment from his robe. "I have full title to these two and the law will back me up."

"Why are they bound?"

"To keep them from running away, of course. Why are slaves collared?"

"Is that why you're driving them like sheep through an alley in the dead of night?"

Farbod used his quirt to tap the shoulder of the smaller of the two females. "You, girl!" he snapped. "Tell him that you two are mine by right."

The girl looked at Artaban, her eyes moist. "It's true," she said in a small voice. "My father died owing this one money, much money. Grandmother and I must serve him until the debt is worked off."

"There!" exulted Farbod. "You see? Now out of our way"

But Artaban didn't answer, for in the silver light of the moon he saw someone he had not seen in more than thirty years: the same dusky skin, the same vibrant eyes and arched brows, the same rose-hued lips and pointed chin. If she removed her head scarf, he knew he would see the same pillowy mass of lustrous black hair she'd once let him glimpse.

Rasha! He beheld his Rasha.

Yet even as he looked on her, he knew it could not be. Rasha was dead. And even alive, she would not be a girl of sixteen.

In his gaze, the  girl saw something that prompted her to speak. "You are the one they call the Mage."

Her question wakened Artaban from his spell. "I am."

"I tell you for the last time," snapped Farbod. "Out of our way."

The girl threw herself at his feet. "Grandmother and I are of the true faith. As a priest of the Holy Fire, save us, O Mage! Save us."

"On your feet," commanded the big man, yanking her rope. The next moment the rope went slack, for Artaban had suddenly drawn the blade from his belt and sliced it in half. The women, their wrists still bound, gasped and huddled together. The big man was about to draw his own knife when he felt a blade at his throat.

"What is your name?" said Artaban, voice full of menace.

"Yashir," he answered hoarsely, the sharp edge pricking his skin.

"Then, Yashir, be still and do nothing rash if you value your life."

"Robbery!" cried Farbod. "You'll regret this! I'll put the law on you and I'll have them back by sunset tomorrow."

"Save your screams," Artaban replied, backing Yashir against a wall. "I'm buying these two, not stealing them."

"Buying?" croaked Farbod. "Are you mad, old man? With what? The girl's worth a small fortune."

"Ismail," said Artaban. "Reach in my belt and get the—"

"I already have it, Master," said Ismail. "But are you sure?"

"Sure?" said Artaban as he plucked Yashir's own knife from his belt. "No, I'm not sure. Nor was I sure on the road to Borsippa, nor sure in Bethlehem or Alexandria. All I know is I can't stand aside when I can save a life – whatever the cost."

"Would you turn your back on your destiny?"

"This child has a destiny too. Show him the pearl, Ismail."

His eyes on Yashir, Artaban heard Ismail's voice, "Behold, Farbod, and know that the god of wealth has smiled on your miserable head."

Artaban heard Farbod gasp. After a moment of silence, he said, "May I touch it?"

"You may not," said Ismail. "My master has carried this for thirty-three years seeking one worthy of it. You, Farbod, are least worthy of all we have met and I include the camels and donkeys we have ridden along the way. Yet give me that parchment and absolve these women of their debt and this is yours."

"I absolve them," Farbod said quickly. "Their debt is paid."

"What god do you worship?" said Ismail.

"Jehovah, of course. I'm a good Jew."

"Then swear in his name."

"That is a very serious thing you ask of me."

"I do not ask. I require it and may Jehovah's wrath fall on your head if you do not speak true."

Farbod sighed. "In the name of Jehovah on high, these women are free of all debt to me."

"Now hand me the parchment."

"Here. Take it."

"I have the parchment, Master."

"Good," said Artaban.

"Now give me the pearl," demanded Farbod.

"Master," said Ismail. "If you kill the big one, this one will take to his heels. We can free the women and still make the palace in time."

Artaban withdrew his knife from Yashir's throat. "An honest man doesn't play the same game of bones twice, Ismail. Give him the pearl."

"I'm not an honest man."

"You're more honest than you know, old friend. Give it to him."

A moment later, Farbod and Yashir were hurrying down the alley. "I'm rich!" cackled Farbod.

"He is until Yashir takes it from him," said Ismail with a bitter smile. "Much woe I see for whoever has that pearl."

"Hold out your wrists," Artaban told the girl. He sawed at the rope binding her, slowly so he did not cut her. "What is your name, child?"

"Sholah, Master."

He was about to reply when a noise from above made them look up, but it was only a loose roof tile jostled by a cat chasing a rat. Artaban returned his gaze to the rope and continued his work. "Do not call me 'Master,' for no one owns you. You and your grandmother are free."

He sliced the last strand of her rope and it slipped to the ground. She rubbed her wrists and smiled at him. "Thank you… sir."

Artaban gestured at the older woman. "Now you, grandmother."

She stepped to him and held out her wrists. Her face in the moonlight showed a woman of perhaps fifty. Care had scored her forehead and there were laugh lines under her eyes but her lips were full and a warm smile lit her features. Though she'd lost the bloom of youth, she was yet a handsome woman and gazed at him with bold, frank eyes. "You have done a wonderful thing."

"I have done a terrible thing," he replied. He sliced through the last strand. "There. You're free. What is your name?"

She held his eyes in her own, her voice steady. "You know my name." She reached up and undid the scarf that hid her hair. It was thick and black, streaked

# Chapter Eighteen

## The Light

FACES swam in and out of the dark: his mother, merry and plump; singing as she cooked, swatting him when he poked his finger in the dough; his father, big but gentle, helping him into the saddle of his first pony; solemn Jabar, guiding his finger to help him decipher the mysterious markings on the parchment. More faces from the recent past appeared as well: Ismail, Red Khamet and others whose names escaped him.

Finally one face swam into view and lingered. He was middle-aged with a full dark beard. On his breast hung a winged circle of gold. "Can you hear me?" he said to Artaban.

Artaban nodded. "Yes," he said weakly, his mouth dry.

The man gave him water and turned to someone out of sight. "Go tell the others that he's awake. And heat some soup." He reached out his hand and felt Artaban's forehead, then unwound the bandage around his head and applied an ointment. "How do you feel?"

"Weak. Tired."

"What is the last thing you remember?"

"The alley and… Rasha… Rasha! Where is she?"

"Here. You'll see her in a moment."

"What happened?"

"A piece of falling tile. It hit you square on the head." He paused, then went on. "You are an old man and it was– *is* a grievous wound. I am sorry to say you are not likely to recover from it. Forgive me for my bluntness but like you I am a priest of Zoroaster, who taught us to speak the truth to those ready to hear it. My name is Rhodaspes. Like you, I have been doctor to many and it's my belief that when time is short, candor is kind. You have lingered at the edge of death for three full days and nights. I have done for you all I can and to be honest, I had given up hope you would open your eyes, much less speak. Praise to the One for letting you climb out of the valley of dreams."

"Praise to him who sets all things in motion and ends our days. Where am I?"

"In my house. Rasha and her granddaughter worship at my temple, as did Sholah's worthy father before he died. When she brought news their freedom had been purchased, I went to see what I could do for you and had you taken here."

"Thank you."

"I am honored. I am proud to be a priest of Zoroaster but for what you have done, three times prouder."

"I do not think you would be so proud if you knew what my kindness has cost the world."

"Your servant told me. The Galilean is dead but you would have not saved him in any case. He had been moved to Herod's dungeon before your friends ever got to Caiaphas's palace."

"The burden this lifts from me is light compared to the heaviness I feel for his loss. He was stoned?"

Rhodaspes bowed his head. "The Romans put him on the cross. Sometimes I am ashamed to be a man." He looked up and a smile lit his face as young Sholah came running in.

"You are awake!" she chirped. "Oh, I am so glad!" She leaned over to kiss Artaban on the cheek. "Oh, Uncle Artaban, every night I have prayed you would open your eyes!"

"'Uncle' am I?" said Artaban. "I could not wish for a sweeter niece but child, sadly, we are not kin."

"You are my uncle in spirit and always will be and that is what I am going to call you!"

"Be glad to be called 'Uncle,'" said Ismail as he came through the door. "She will not even call me 'Cousin' for fear others might think her related to someone so homely." He reached down and clasped Artaban's hand tightly. "We found the babe, Master. A pity we found him too late. Are you hungry?"

"A little, yes."

"Rasha is coming with soup." He turned to the girl. "Sholah, help me raise Uncle Artaban so he can sit up."

Once Artaban was repositioned and made comfortable, Rhodaspes led the others out. "He is weak and we must not overtire him. Let her get some food into him." They left as Rasha entered with a bowl of steaming broth.

"There you are, Greybeard!" she said merrily. "I hope you're hungry, because I intend for you to eat every bite of this. It will bring your strength back."

"Hungry I am," he replied, "but more than that, I am thirsty."

She sat on the edge of the bed, the bowl in her lap. "Do you want a drink of water?"

"For my throat and stomach, the soup will be enough. It is my heart that is thirsty. For more than thirty years, it has done without grace and beauty, and now that I see you I would drink you with my eyes day and night and still be unquenched."

She lifted a spoonful of broth to his mouth. "Oh, you are a silver-tongued old rogue! Do you think to turn my head with such nonsense?"

He swallowed the soup, which was hot and salty and tasted of celery and chicken. "It is the truth."

She laughed. "Why spoil flattery with truth? I am a grey-haired old widow woman but in my heart I'm still a foolish girl, eager as ever to be praised and adored. Open your mouth." He swallowed another spoonful and she continued. "Ismail has been telling me of your wanderings. I thought *I* was a traveler but I haven't been to half the places you have."

"I was in Alexandria, about to return to Ecbatana when I met Hamid. He told me you had died of a fever."

She gave him another spoon and snorted. "That is the story my father put out. He couldn't stand the humiliation of a rebellious daughter."

"What do you mean?"

"Open your mouth. I ran away."

Artaban nearly choked on his soup. "Ran away? With a man?"

She glowered at him. "No, you fool of a greybeard. I ran away to find *you*."

"Me?"

"After three months I could wait no longer. I feared it would be years before you returned. Or worse, return with a wife you'd acquired in Egypt or Babylon."

"I swore I'd return. Why couldn't you wait?"

"Because I was sixteen and at sixteen a month is a year and three months is a lifetime and I was in love with my dark, handsome, arrogant Mage!"

"You went looking for me? How did you live?"

"By my wits and by whatever god looks after fools. I cut my hair and pretended to be a boy."

"Cut your hair!"

"Open your mouth. It grew back but I must say I convinced more than a few. A boy who was a player with a band of mummers befriended me. I joined them."

"And you never went back to Ecbatana?"

"Not for years. And then I left again. That was after Jabar had sold your house. He told me where Ismail had gone and I went to Greece but of course the two of you were long gone. I would have kept looking but, well, I was with child and then I was married and my husband and I had a bakery to run. Open your mouth."

So it went and by the time the bowl was empty, Artaban knew the names of her first husband and her second and those of her children and grandchildren. He was weary but happier than he'd been in years.

She nestled beside him on the bed for a while and when his head nodded, fluffed his pillows and told him to close his eyes; she would be back when he'd napped.

When he woke, he ate another bowl of soup, this time fed him by Sholah. "Uncle Artaban," she said. "I am so sorry you didn't get to talk to the Galilean. You would have liked him. We did."

"You saw him?"

"Yes, in Safed. A friend of Papa's told us about him. Papa had business there and took us with him. We went to the market and heard him. He spoke so well and made everything so plain! Grandmother was very taken with him and she is not someone easily impressed. She says the world is full of fools and frauds."

"I suppose it is," said Artaban. "But there are wise men as well. One must learn to tell the difference."

"Ismail says you are the wisest man he has ever known."

"Ismail is almost as great a fool as I am."

"Who calls you a fool, Uncle? I know you are brave and Rhodaspes says you are very learned. Ismail says you have a magic looker that makes the stars come close. May I look through it some night?"

Artaban sighed. "It is not magic but yes, you may look through it, perhaps tonight if I can stand. It will have to be some night soon for I don't think I have many ahead of me."

"Don't talk like that, Uncle! You have long years ahead of you."

"Well, perhaps I do," he said soothingly. "No more soup, Sholah. I'm full." He heard noise in the street, people shouting, someone loudly weeping, someone else laughing. "What is that commotion outside?"

"I don't know," said the girl. "Do you want me to find out?"

Artaban nodded and she left. A few moments later she returned. "I'm not sure what it's about. I heard someone say 'he's risen,' but I don't know what—" She fell silent when she saw that Artaban was asleep.

THE NEXT time he woke it was afternoon. Ismail was seated beside him. He gave his master a drink of water and checked his bandages. Artaban heard Ismail ask if he was hungry but he was too tired to answer. He drifted off and when he opened his eyes again it was dusk and Rasha sat in the chair. She asked him if he needed anything and he shook his head. He felt her take his hand in hers, her grasp warm and tender and perfectly fitted to his hand.

When he next woke it was dark. A candle flickered low in a corner of the room. Someone was in the chair and as his eyes adjusted he could tell it was a man, not young but not yet in middle age. He had a fair face and dark brown beard and wore a white robe. "You've been long asleep," he said with a smile.

"I'm thirsty," Artaban answered.

The man took a jug and poured a cup of water, which he held to Artaban's lips. It was cool and soothing and he drank long. "I don't know you," he said when he was done. "Are you a new servant?"

"A servant, yes," the other answered, "but not to this house. And you do know me. You have known me almost all my life, but now we finally meet."

Artaban silently studied the man by the dancing candle light. His intelligent eyes were brown and free of guile and they met Artaban's gaze openly. At last the Mage said, "I was told you died."

"So I did."

"I have never beheld a spirit before. Am I dead?"

"You are quite alive and I am not a spirit. I am flesh and bone as much as you." He held out his hand and Artaban gripped it. It was solid and warm. Artaban felt wetness and when he let go, he saw there was blood on his palm. "I had gifts for you," he said. "Three. Now I have none."

"You gave them away."

"Yes."

"And I accepted them gladly. You healed me and defended me and bought my freedom."

"I don't understand."

"All the people of earth are my children and whatever you do for them—for the least of them—you do for me."

"I sought to do more. I sought to save you."

"That was not my destiny, so it could not be yours."

"But I have nothing to give you now."

"You have lived your life selflessly serving others and never faltered in your quest. That is more than enough gift for me."

"Yet I wish I had something."

"Well," said the man with a slight hesitation. "There is one thing."

"Name it."

He pointed at Artaban's brass cylinder, which lay on a nearby table. "You have a magic looker that makes the stars come close."

"It isn't..." Artaban began, then sighed. "Yes, I do."

"Will you show me?"

"Gladly," smiled Artaban. "If you'll help me outside." He sat up and slid his legs off the bed. He felt surprisingly strong and though he had to lean on the man, they left the house and went into a small green garden where they sat on a stone bench.

The moon was down and the sky glittered with pricks of light. Artaban extended the cylinder to its full length and handed it to the young man. "Hold the glass with your right hand. Close one eye and put the narrow end to the other."

The man did as instructed. "What do you see?" Artaban asked.

"Bright light everywhere."

"There is a raised knob of sorts in the middle. Use your free hand to turn it slowly. The light will resolve into individual stars."

After a few seconds, the man gave a small gasp. "But this is wonderful! When I was little, my father—I mean Joseph—used to take me out at night and point out the stars. He would name them and tell me 'star stories,' you know, tales of heroes and dragons. I loved that but this, this is more marvelous still. So bright!" After another silence, he asked. "That big one, do you know its name?"

"Where?"

"There. That bright one in the sign of the dragon."

"Let me see." Artaban took the glass and peered through it. "That is… that is… no, it cannot be!"

He removed the glass and turned to his companion. "It is the wandering star, the one I followed to Bethlehem." He turned his eyes back to the heavens. The star shone with a radiant, constant light, now so bright he saw it without the telescope. "It's back! Where has it been?"

"It has always been there," said Jesus. He rose and kissed Artaban on the forehead. "But only those of perfect faith can see it."

Dawn came an hour later and they found him in the garden beside the bench. He lay on his back, the glass in one hand, his eyes open and unseeing but wide, as if with wonder.

*Here ends the tale of the Last Magi, both the most foolish and wisest of that order. Go, seeker. The way may be unsure and dark but only at night do we see the stars. Look to the heavens and find your own. Have faith and follow it, even if no one can see its light but you.*

The End

Thank you for reading *The Last Magi*. I hope you enjoyed it! If you're interested in Rasha's tale or have a comment for the author, you can contact me at:

<u>WordSharpe@gmail.com</u>

E.A. Sharpe is a Texas writer who has written plays, screenplays, novels, documentaries, magazine articles, reviews, newspaper columns, websites, advertisements, commercials, infomercials, letters to the editor and occasional postcards. He can be contacted at WordSharpe@gmail.com.

<u>Credits</u>: Cover art by Robin of
designmediaservices2@gmail.com

Special thanks to friend and
Publisher Extraordinaire, Bill Benitez
Of Positive Imaging, LLC, for
Shepherding this book to print

37076766R00110

Made in the USA
Middletown, DE
19 November 2016